PRESSING ADALYN

Jenn Hype

Pressing Adalyn

ISBN-13: 978-0-692-51701-7
ISBN-10: 0-692-51701-4

Book design by J. F. Rountree
Cover photograph © Aleshyn_Andrei/ShutterStock.com

www.jennhype.com
press@jennhype.com

First Edition August 2015

Printed in the United States of America
10 9 8 7 6 5 4 3 2 1

For someone
Just because

CHAPTER 1

"Shit!" I heard someone yell from one of the dorm rooms down the hall. A long string of curse words followed, most of which I wouldn't even feel comfortable repeating. And to my horror, as I approached the room where the yelling was coming from, I realized that it was, in fact, my dorm room.

And that blonde cursing out an empty room, yeah that was my new roommate, Stacy.

"Um, excuse me? Are you Stacy?" I asked, my voice sounding a little more hesitant than I had intended, but I had to live with this girl for the next year so I figured I should approach her delicately. I didn't want to end up on the receiving end of whatever had gotten her so angry.

"Yeah, who the hell wants to know?" she replied without even turning around to face me.

"I'm Adalyn, your new roommate." I walked toward her, my hand outstretched in greeting and stood there for what felt like several minutes. As she finally turned around to face me, she just looked down at my hand and back up at me and without another word walked out of the room.

I quickly threw my bags on the empty bed, which I

assumed was mine, and chased after her.

"Wait! Where are you going? I thought maybe we could get to know each other a little bit since we're going to spend so much time together over the next year."

She stopped so abruptly that I almost crashed into her.

"Look, Avery."

"Um, it's Adalyn."

"Whatever…. Adalyn. I'm having a bad fucking day, okay? I don't have time to sit around and braid your hair and play twenty questions or do whatever form of female bonding shit you thought was going to happen. If you hadn't noticed, I spilled my entire latte all down the front of my shirt. See?" she said, gesturing at a big brown splotch on her white blouse - a splotch that was now dripping down onto her jeans.

"I'm sorry. I didn't even notice. You had your back to me. Do you need help?"

"Do I need…" she sighed impatiently and muttered something under her breath that sounded a lot like "dumb bitches," as she massaged her temples.

"No, I don't need your help wiping off my shirt. I'm perfectly capable of using a towel. I also know how to use a spoon and put my own clothes on in the morning, so you won't have to help with any of that shit, either. Just to clear that up for you before you offer."

She turned around again and stormed off, still mumbling under her breath.

I walked back to our dorm room and sat on my empty bed trying to figure out what the hell had just happened. At first I ran through the events that led up to her leaving, trying to figure out if I had said or done something offensive in that exchange that would have caused her to act so rudely towards me. But the more I thought about it, the more I realized I hadn't done anything wrong. She was just being a bitch. And if I was going to be stuck in this room with someone as hateful as her, I needed to make sure she understood that I wasn't going to put up with her treating me like shit all the time.

So, being the immature brat that I was, I completely stripped her bedding, wadded it up and threw it out the door into the hallway. That was quickly followed by an armful of her clothes. She returned to the room just as I was getting another armful of clothes and she yanked on my shoulder, causing me to stumble backwards and drop everything to the ground.

"What the hell do you think you're doing!", she screamed at me, getting entirely too close to my face. I did *not* like people in my personal space. So I pushed her with both hands as hard as I could and she tripped over the pile of clothes I had just dropped and landed hard on her ass.

I tried hard not to laugh. I really did. But I couldn't help it. The shock and anger on her face was hysterical.

"What's it look like I'm doing? I'm helping you move out." Confusion joined the mix of emotions being displayed on her face, but I kept going before she could interrupt. "There is no way I'm putting up with being treated like crap all year, and because I'm a nice person, I decided to help you pack. So if you don't mind, I'm going to finish getting all of your crap out of *my* dorm room," I said as I made my way back to the closet to get more of her clothes.

I'd only made it a few steps when she reached out and grabbed me by the ankle, causing me to lunge forward. I regained my balance just in time, preventing myself from going all the way down. She didn't give me much time to recover from almost falling though, because as soon as I stood upright, she tackled me.

We continued to struggle, rolling around on the ground, pulling each other's hair and trying unsuccessfully to slap each other. At some point a crowd had gathered just outside our door and several girls were laughing while the boys were chanting "girl fight" over and over.

Just as I bit down on Stacy's forearm, she got a good jab into my eye with her elbow. It was utterly ridiculous. Neither of us was really making any progress in hurting the other, we mostly just took turns rolling on top of each other, somersaulting all across the room.

Finally, when we were both so winded from fighting, the Resident Assistant showed up. She broke up the crowd and started yelling loudly, pulling us out of our rage-induced cat fight. We both paused at the same time, my right hand tangled in her hair with my left hand wrapped tightly around her wrist. She had both of her legs wrapped around my waist and she was pushing my face away with the palm of her free hand.

The look on the RA's face was sheer terror. Stacy and I looked at each other and after a long pause, we broke into a hysterical fit of laughter. Our now irritated RA huffed out of the room, grumbling about us being immature children, and Stacy and I just continued to crack up over how ridiculous we must have looked in that moment. We untangled ourselves from each other and gripped hands, pulling one another up, then reintroduced ourselves.

"Do over?" I asked.

"You got it, whore."

And that's how I met my best friend.

Chapter 2

"Hurry up and finish getting ready, whore. We have a ton of shit to do today before the party tonight."

Yep. Six years later and my best friend hadn't changed a bit.

"Shut up, Stacy. I already don't feel like going out tonight and your friends are bitches. I am way too exhausted to have to put up with people I don't like, especially at a club. There probably won't be anywhere to sit and I'll end up whining the whole time and making you regret that you bothered to force me to go out with you in the first place."

I already knew she wasn't going to let me off the hook. I'd packed up and moved across several states to live with her over a month ago and I still hadn't even attempted to go out and see the city. There were a few times she dragged me out to local clubs or bars, but I hadn't been good company.

Recently having made the decision to forgo any kind of physical or emotional relationship with men had me avoiding them like the plague. So whereas normally I would be out dancing, stealing the mic from the DJ or generally throwing myself at a hot stranger, now I was a self declared wall fly. Hunkering in a corner, simply there to observe and be the designated driver.

I don't drink. Haven't since college. Nothing against drinking, I just have control issues. When I say control issues, I mean in every aspect of my life. I don't give in to peer pressure, or pressure of any kind for that matter. Nothing will make me act out or behave irrationally more than someone trying to tell me what to do. These control issues have caused problems in almost every facet of my life, but I've come to terms with this and am in no hurry to change.

Unfortunately, 'annoyingly stubborn' and 'irritatingly difficult' apparently can't be listed under 'skill set' on your resume. At least not if you actually want the job. So since graduating college with some bs degree because I never could decide on a major, I've bounced around between one shitty job to the next. I'm very smart, easy on the eyes and a quick learner. However, none of that overshadows my uncanny ability to piss off my bosses. Did you know that there is no job that exists out there where you get to call all the shots and boss people around without actually being the boss? Go figure.

I've also never stayed at a job long enough to be able to work my way into a management position. Not that time would make a difference, because I will never kiss ass to get higher up in a company. I'd rather suck an egg. Plus, even managers have bosses. Being homeless, wandering the city, having to answer to no one was actually a tempting concept on some days. Of course I would never actually do that, but it was nice to dream.

Dream of being homeless? Now that was just sad...

I've also found out over the last few years that men hate being bossed around as much as I do. I guess not holding a steady job, never letting your date decide where you're going for the night and refusing to let the man have any control in bed is not really what most men are looking for in a woman. Never mind the fact that I'm intelligent, have great tits and killer legs and could rival the best of them in a game of darts. The movies and books are lying, ladies. That bullshit where the guy likes a woman with a mind of her own, who is beautiful and acts like one of the guys is just lies. LIES, I TELL YOU! I'm lucky to make it past the second date.

Yeah, men act like they want a gorgeous woman who can eat her weight in steak, watches sports and act like one of the guys while still keeping up in an intellectual conversation. That may be true, but they also want this woman to laugh at all of their jokes even if they aren't funny, swoon over any romantic gesture they make, no matter how lame it is, and to constantly praise them and validate their egos.

I'm happy to be the first part of that description, straight up refuse the latter. If I can't find a man who appreciates my extreme honesty, even if it's at their expense, then I'd rather be alone. And I'm damn sure never going to give anyone praise they don't deserve. Remember how I said I wouldn't kiss my boss's ass? That really applies to everyone.

On top of all my domineering qualities, I'm also picky as hell. Yeah, I could probably find a guy to put up with me. I've actually found quite a few. However, they were all weak minded, insecure man- children who couldn't find my clit even if a giant neon sign were pointing directly at it.

Just because I can't find a man who I feel is actually deserving of my time who will stick around long enough to look past some of my overbearing personality traits, doesn't mean I'm willing to just drop my standards entirely. Winning an argument isn't fun if the person doesn't even try to argue back. What's the fun in winning if your opponent could care less if they won or not? And I'm very competitive about literally everything.

I'm so competitive that no one will play anything with me, no matter what it is. Board games, video games, cards, pool... doesn't matter what it is. If in the end someone will be declared a winner, then all of a sudden no one is "in the mood" to play. Wusses.

It took a couple of years, lots of therapy and several memories I wish I could forget, for me to discover all of this about myself. Becoming more self aware actually made it worse in the beginning, because my ways of coping were more than unhealthy. I was still trying to figure out a happy medium but compromising, even with myself, was never my strong suit. I was working on it though. Well...kind of...

Yeah, there was a brief time in my life where all of this was depressing. A *VERY* brief time. I'm not one to sit around and wallow and feel sorry for myself. So after several failed attempts at dating, I had decided being in a relationship could be put on hold. I needed to figure out my own crap anyway. Maybe if I at least held a steady job then I might be able to keep the attention of someone I was actually interested in.

So... since I'd pretty much exhausted most of my employment opportunities back home in Ohio, I called up Stacy and asked if she would like a roommate. I took the shrieking on the other end of the phone as a yes, and a week later I had packed up everything I would need to start over with my best friend in New York.

Stacy, God love her. She was a firecracker and keeping up with her was difficult. She'd been putting up with my grumpy ass for over a month now. Getting her to stay still for more than five minutes was exhausting and it tested my patience constantly. She was always looking for a good time, and right now I just wanted to take a step back and be with myself for a while. Getting her to listen to me and accept that that's what I needed right now was driving me out of my ever-loving-mind.

Despite all of this, I was beyond excited to be living with my best friend again. We'd kept in touch after I moved back home when we graduated. Stacy was from New York, so staying here was just a given for her, but I had no idea what I was doing with my life so I thought going home would be the mature decision. Take some time to figure it out. Moving home, however, only made it worse. I felt like a loser. I was still depending on my parents, and barely able to pay my own cell phone bill since I was constantly between jobs.

I had originally come to New York for school because of their art program. Plans changed though after freshman year and when it came time to declare a major, I had already missed so much school and was dealing with so many personal issues that I just picked a generic business degree.... even though I had no desire to work in any type of office setting. I had dreamt my whole life of doing something with art. I had foolishly convinced myself that I could find a way to transfer my passion for art into an actual job, either by doing design work or actually getting paid to commission my own works.

Fail.

Stacy had been my rock and main source of moral support since we'd met. She had always stood behind me no matter what decisions I made, but she wasn't afraid to let me know if my decisions were stupid, either. And despite how wild she was and how far out of my comfort zone she forced me, she was the only one who knew my history. She knew all of the reasons I was so messed up and why I didn't drink alcohol.

When I did manage to force myself to go out with Stacy, I always ended up having a good time. Stacy was already a loose cannon, but when she was drinking it was hilarious. Every time we went out she made a complete ass out of herself. As much as I tried to use the multitude of stories, videos and pictures against her, it never worked. I'd never met someone who cared so little about what other people thought. To her, the more embarrassing the story, the more entertaining...even if it was at her expense.

Because I loved Stacy and she was one of my only friends in the city, I gave in to her relentless nagging and finally agreed to go out. One of Stacy's friends knew the owner of some nightclub that was opening up and had gotten us VIP status for the night. Stacy had been dying to go. I was less than thrilled at the thought of a night out with her and her friends. Stacy's friend Carrie, in particular, whom she'd known since she was four years old was the worst. I had a sneaking suspicion that Carrie hated me, though I had no idea why. She hadn't been rude, at least not in an obvious way, but every time I was around she just glared at me and no matter how much I tried to engage her in conversation she barely responded. So I just started avoiding her, though my efforts were futile considering how close she was with Stacy.

Stacy had warned me about Carrie before I moved in with her. She didn't go into detail about the reasons behind Carrie's personality, but she made it clear that I was to take it easy and back off. I *may* or *may not* have a tendency to be pretty confrontational at times. I also *may* or *may not* struggle with having a filter for my thoughts. Apparently this Carrie chick was sensitive or some shit and Stacy was afraid I would cause drama. I didn't need that crap right now anyway. I had tried being nice and it wasn't working, so avoiding her was the next best option.

Having to be around Carrie while simultaneously trying to avoid her still wasn't the worst part, though. Nope, the worst part was where we were going. The opening of this club had been talked about for weeks in the paper and on the local news. The name of this highly anticipated club? Grind. Yeah you heard me. The name of the club was *Grind*. I was sure it would be true to it's name. Why? Because what do drunk boys do at clubs? They grind up against drunk girls. Or sober girls. Or anything with an orifice they can stick their dick into…no matter how unwanted their attention was.

Joy.

Not only did I not need the temptation of hot, sweaty men grinding against my leg, but since this was the opening night for this club and it was supposed to be an ultra exclusive, high profile type of ordeal, it was sure to be packed. Word was it was going to be filled with the city's most gorgeous and eligible bachelors, so yep... tonight was going to be torturous.

"I know what you're thinking, Adalyn...yes, it's probably going to be packed and I know you've been completely anti-social lately, but the security is being doubled since it's opening night and because they want the club to have a more exclusive feel so they aren't going to put up with the usual drunken dumbasses that you would see in an average club."

"That's not the point, Stacy. Yeah, I really don't want some drunk guy rubbing up against me, but I especially don't want extremely hot and successful ones doing it, either. I'm celibate right now. I don't want or need the temptation."

She actually had no idea just how long it had been since I'd had 'intimate relations' with a man. Let's just say it had been a really long time. Embarrassingly long.

"I wish you would just let loose tonight, Addy. I won't drink. I'll watch you and be the responsible one for once. You can dance and have a good time and I'll scare off any men that approach you." Stacy's pleading eyes made me feel horribly guilty because I knew she only wanted what was best for me, but I knew letting go would be a mistake.

"Stacy, I know you would do that for me and you

are the only one I would trust to make sure I didn't do something incredibly stupid, but I really have no desire to drink or do anything outside of just hanging out. I'll be fine, I promise."

I could see the disappointment in her face and for a brief moment I almost contemplated her offer. That thought quickly vanished as reality set in and reminded me of how incredibly stupid it would be. I wished we were going somewhere smaller or more relaxed. A comedy club, a karaoke bar, hell even a strip club would be better. Those environments were much more controlled and the chances of the men attending said places actually being hot enough to tempt me were pretty low.

Maybe it wasn't too late. Maybe I could still find a way out of going. Stacy had other friends that would be there so it wasn't like me not being there would ruin anything. I was wracking my brain, trying to come up with a way to back out without pissing her off. Maybe there was some old sushi I could dig out of a trash can and eat so I could give myself food poisoning. Sadly, that alternative was much more appealing than going dancing.

Right on cue, as if reading my thoughts, Stacy started in. "No matter what you're feeling right now, you HAVE to go. If I don't get laid soon, my vagina will shrivel up and die. I can't neglect her any longer."

"Stacy, it's only been a week since you had sex. Quit being such a slut. If your vagina needs some attention, then let Gerard take care of her." Gerard is what Stacy had affectionately named her giant dildo. Giant is really an understatement. More like terrifying. I mean, how did she even get it in there? You know what. Never mind. So not an image I needed to picture.

"Gerard just hasn't been cutting it lately. I don't know if it's him or Jay-Jay, but they just aren't jiving and I can tell the little lady is starting to grow some serious animosity towards me and when she gets cranky, I get cranky. Besides…I just had her groomed and she wants to show off her new hair-do."

"Seriously Stacy, quit talking about your vagina like she's an actual person. It's freaking weird. Sometimes I seriously wonder if you should be medicated."

"Pfffft. You know you love my crazy."

"Yeah, yeah," I mumbled as I headed to my closet to pick out something casual to wear for our errands today. It was rainy and tonight was going to be exhausting, so I was planning on going completely casual and comfortable. Slipping on a pair of skinny jeans, pink ballerina flats and a pink long sleeved tee, I threw my hair up in a messy bun and headed towards the bathroom.

I was not one of those girls who looked pretty without make up. Splotchy skin, and circles under my eyes. Without eyeliner and mascara, I looked half asleep. I'd spent a lot of time in my life wishing to be one of those naturally beautiful women. I had tried every beauty product known to man, but was never able to achieve an effortless beauty. So up until five years ago, there was never a time where I would even entertain the possibility of leaving my bedroom without a stitch of makeup on. Going outside nude would be less embarrassing. Okay, maybe not less, but you get it.

Now things were different though. Don't get me wrong, I cared about how I looked. And it's not like I had a hairy mole or a goiter or any serious flaws. Even without makeup I could pass for "pretty", I just wasn't naturally stunning. The difference now was that I had enough self esteem to not constantly worry about what other people were thinking about me. If someone didn't like what they saw, then look away. I stopped living my life for others a long time ago.

My hair laid several inches past my shoulders, it's natural color of a dark brown. Depending on the clothes I wore, I could usually keep a low profile. I was no supermodel by any means, but I knew I looked good naked. I just didn't want to go around flaunting my body at all times. While I loved being the center of attention, it had to be on my terms and when I felt in the mood for it. Dressing modestly and not dolling myself up allowed me to stay hidden for the most part until I wanted to be seen. Dressing up and looking nice was something I only did for myself, not for someone else.

I brushed my teeth and splashed some water on my

face, deciding to forgo the make up. My how times have changed. It was painful to think about my life before, in more ways than one. Sometimes I didn't even recognize the person looking back at me. So I shoved those memories back down where I kept them. Deep down in the seedy underbelly that is my past.

Pulling myself out of my trance and forcing a smile on my face I walked up to Stacy. "Alright, dickwad. Let's get this day over with."

CHAPTER 3

ADALYN

"Why the hell did I move out here? I hate this city. It's too loud and there are too many people. Why is everyone here so rude!? Would it kill someone to say 'excuse me' once in a while? Seriously! And now, it's freaking raining. No, correction, pissing all over us like it's intentionally navigating away from our umbrella just to smack me in the face."

"Would you stop your freaking bitching and just relax for once in your life and quit acting like a prissy twat. If I didn't love your face so much I'd fucking punch it right now," Stacy snapped at me.

I deserved it. We'd been out running errands for only an hour and I hadn't stopped complaining since the moment we walked out the door. It's not that I hated the rain, I didn't care about getting wet, it was having to walk around the city in soaking wet jeans and water filled shoes just to be dragged into high end boutiques where they stared at you like you were a homeless person who wandered in off the street that really bothered me. *Freaking judgmental bitches.*

Since I rarely went out anymore and Stacy deemed our girls' night at the club a "special occasion" she had insisted I find something nice to wear. Based on the dresses she made me try, it became obvious that the dress code was "slutty." I wasn't self conscious about my body, but I didn't want to be drawing attention to myself, either. The goal for tonight was to try to have fun while remaining inconspicuous, not flash my lady bits to every man within a ten-foot radius.

"I need a break, Stacy. I'm hungry and tired and I need to dry off. Get some caffeine in me and I'll be in a better mood. Not a good mood, but a better one," I pleaded, clasping my hands together as if in prayer and giving her my best pouty face. I was not above begging when it came to caffeine.

"Fine. I need to stop by Carrie's work first to drop something off to her and then we can head to the sandwich shop and take a break. But then I swear to all things holy, if you do not perk up and cooperate after that, I will seriously cunt punch you."

She meant it. She had done it before. I cringed at the memory.

Grumbling under my breath, I followed her to Carrie's work. Freaking Carrie. I shouldn't hold such animosity towards her since I've never even really had a full conversation with her. She just rubbed me the wrong way, I couldn't help it. Okay, I could help it if I really tried but I didn't want to try.

Next thing I knew, we were walking up the steps to some huge, fancy ass building. The entire front side of the tall building was made up of windows. They were slightly tinted so you couldn't see inside very well, but I imagined at night you could see almost everything.

When we opened the doors and walked in I immediately felt uncomfortable. Everything looked so...clean. Sharp edges, shiny surfaces, ridiculous art sculptures that looked like heaps of metal that had been rescued from the dump. I hated it. I lived my life in color. Warm, bright and creative environments are what I felt most comfortable in. I couldn't wait to get out of this corporate prison. It's no wonder Carrie worked here, seeing as how her personality was as cold and rigid as the building.

Stacy started to walk up to a woman sitting behind a large desk, but when she began to speak, a tall man appearing out of nowhere interrupted her. I turned slightly, pulling my eyes off of the hideous art, only to be faced with the most beautiful creature I had ever seen. Yes, creature, because there was no way the man standing in front of me was an actual human being. Maybe a mirage? I *was* really hungry. Maybe my blood sugar had dropped so low that I was hallucinating sex gods.

As I neared where Stacy and the sex god were standing, I realized I wasn't unconscious and only dreaming about the delicious man candy in front of me. Nope, he was real. I could reach out and touch him if I wanted to. And I *really* wanted to. But I didn't. I don't know how I managed to keep my hands to myself, but I did. Go me!

He had to be at least 6'3", maybe taller. Dark hair, a little longer on the top, perfect for running your fingers through. Dark eyes that could weaken the knees of all womankind and intimidate even the most powerful men. Chiseled, sharp features defined a face that, if he were scowling, would make him extremely terrifying, but he was smiling. A small dimple on his left cheek made his gorgeous face look more than adorable.

I'm pretty sure I died for a couple of minutes. Someone should have checked my pulse, or given me CPR. I'm confident that I stopped breathing. I'd never seen someone so perfect in real life. I literally wiped drool from my chin. Yep. I was drooling. Luckily no one was paying attention to me. How could they? The example of magical, manly perfection that was standing before me had pulled everyone's attention right to him, and I was pretty sure I wasn't the only one drooling.

And yes, you heard me right. *Magical*. The only way a man could be this stunningly perfect would be from the assistance of some kind of fairy god mother or a higher being.

Oh shit, I'd been standing there staring for God knows how long. Being caught staring was enough to make me feel embarrassed and vulnerable, especially when I noticed the smirk on his face. I only felt like an idiot for about two seconds though. Any time I felt any sort of 'weak' emotion I quickly replaced it with anger and bitchiness, a defense mechanism I had perfected over the years that ended up biting me in the ass every single time, but I was too stubborn to change.

I forced myself to tear my eyes away from his body, mostly because if I didn't then I wouldn't be able to stop trying to picture him naked. His eyes seemed like a safer option. So I looked up at him, right into his soul searching, will power devouring, panty dropping eyes. I was strong, I could resist him. Or at the very least, I was good at pretending.

That's right, buddy. I'm immune to your tricks. I know I don't know him, but I know guys like him. They know exactly how sexy they are and they think they can melt the panties right off of any woman they deem worthy of their charm. And let's be real, if I wasn't so messed up, my panties wouldn't have melted, they would have gone up in flames. Unfortunately for him, my panties were fireproof when it came to his kind. No matter how devastatingly handsome they were.

Go ahead, slick, give it your best shot. Flash me those pearly whites.

Right on cue, he flashed me a grin that probably would have most women creaming their pants on the spot, as he held his hand out, expecting me to grab on for a friendly shake. I'm sure he thought that as soon as we touched I would swoon. Probably expected me to sigh dreamily and flutter my eyelashes at him. So despite my raising body temperature, shaky legs and quivering sex, I did what I do best.

I made everything awkward.

CHAPTER 4

IAN

"Yeah, I'm not touching that." It took a second for me to realize the gorgeous woman who had just walked up behind Stacy was actually talking to me. *Touch what? Oh, my hand.* I lowered my arm back to my side and tilted my head, studying her face and trying to get a read on whether or not she was joking. She wasn't smiling and her stance was pretty rigid, so if she wasn't being serious then she had one hell of a poker face. She turned away from me to look at Stacy. "Are we done here yet, Stace?" she asked Stacy impatiently.

Well… that's certainly a new reaction. Not every woman I flashed my smile at fainted at my feet, begging to have my babies, but certainly none of them have ever looked at me like I'm insane. Or refused to shake my hand as if they might catch some kind of disease from touching me.

Her clothes were wet from being out in the spontaneous rain storm we'd just had. Her thin shirt clung to her body, defining the lacy bra she was wearing and giving me a good visual of her hard nipples. Her flat stomach tapered into low rise, tight fitting jeans that hugged her in all the right places. Her long, dark hair was pulled up into a ponytail, showing off her slender neck and her beautiful face. Her hair was still dry, probably the only part of her protected by the umbrella, and it looked amazingly soft. I wondered what it would feel like between my fingers, wrapped around my fist as we kissed.

"Excuse me," I spoke up, shaking the naughty fantasy that was progressing in my thoughts before I did something to embarrass myself, like get a hard on in front of the woman standing before me who was, hands down, the most beautiful woman I'd ever met. She whipped her head back towards me and narrowed her eyes.

"I didn't mean to interrupt. I'll wait for you outside, Stacy." She gave me a once over, but not in an appreciative way. In fact, she was looking at me like she found me to be repulsive.

What. The. Fuck. Did I slip into some alternate universe where women suddenly hated a man in an expensive tailor made suit and a two-hundred-dollar haircut? Those things didn't really matter to me, it was just part of my persona, a part I was playing when I had to be in business owner mode. But in my experience, those things were important to women. Well, except for this one apparently.

"No, I apologize, I wasn't implying you were interrupting. I just wanted to introduce myself. I'm Ian Drake, and you are?" I asked as nicely as I could while being stared down by the she-devil herself.

She snorted then rolled her eyes again. Had Stacy

been talking shit about me or something? Were there rumors circulating about me that I was unaware of? How could someone I'd never met have so much disdain for me.

"Eh hem." Stacy cleared her throat and took a step closer to me, making herself somewhat of a physical barrier between me and her friend. "Anyway, Ian this is Adalyn Montgomery. She's the one I told you about that might be good for that position that's open at your office. Although, if the past few minutes are any indication, I'm thinking you two are better off staying far away from each other."

"Adalyn! She has a name. It's nice to meet you, Adalyn." I smiled sweetly at her and held out my hand again. She still didn't take it. Instead she turned to face Stacy again, her face turning red and her knuckles white from clenching her hands into a hard fist.

"What the hell, Stacy," Adalyn growled between clenched teeth. "You didn't tell me anything about recommending me for a job, and besides, why would you think I'd want to work at a place like this?" She gestured around the room with her hand.

"It's a good job, Addy. You should at least hear him out."

"No, no way. I'm not working at this...this...this... place. I just won't do it," she huffed.

"I'm sorry. I don't mean to interrupt this private

conversation you two are having in public, but what kind of place do you think this is, Adalyn? I may be a little biased seeing as how I own this company, but I can assure you it's a great place to work. I would love for you to come in one-day next week to discuss the position we are looking to fill. Stacy has assured me you would be a great fit."

"Screw you," she spat back at me. I just stood there, blinking at her, jaw dropped, gaping like an idiot. I must have misheard her. Considering how incredibly rude she had been in the five minutes I'd known her, the fact that I was still willing to consider her for the position was pretty generous, I thought. So surely I had heard her wrong.

"Excuse me?"

"You heard me. Screw you. I'm not desperate enough for a job to work for a cocky, egomaniacal asshole like you. From the past few minutes alone I can already tell that you are arrogant and boring."

"Boring?" I didn't mean to smirk. It was just such an odd accusation. I really didn't think I was *any* of those things, but boring was an especially interesting choice of insult in that moment. I wasn't some cut throat business mogul, working my employees to the bone and treating them like crap. It was actually a really fun, laid back place to work.

"If your building is any indication, yes. Everything in here is cold and hard. Devoid of any personality what-so-ever. Which I take to mean you expect your employees to fall in line and march to your orders, and that will NEVER be me. I can assure you of that. So why don't we cut the bull shit and I'll just lay it out for you. I don't want the job and I'm not going to buy your act so you're wasting your time."

Feigning injury and covering my heart with my hand, I stumbled backward, pretending as if I'd just taken a hit. "You wound me, Adalyn. And here, I thought we had a connection. I may have to cancel tonight Stacy since I'll be too busy licking my wounds. Unless, of course, you'd like to lick them for me," I said to Adalyn with a wink. That earned me an eye roll.

"No, you're going to spend all night partying your ass off with me. You had better be there tonight, Ian, or I will personally kick your ass. And you know me, that is not an empty threat," Stacy chimed in as she smacked me on the arm.

I chuckled. "As bossy as ever, Stacy. Yes, I will be there. Unfortunately, though, none of my single friends were available to tag along so I won't be able to provide your entertainment for the evening."

"Dammit," Stacy said, pouting and stomping her foot.

"Great. As if tonight wasn't going to be bad enough...." I heard Adalyn mumble under her breath.

"Don't worry, sunshine. I'll keep you company. I'll

bet I can even get you to loosen up a bit."

"Ugh, so full of yourself. Like I would ever want your company. I'd rather be groped by a gang of greasy, fat bikers than spend any amount of time with you."

And with that, she turned and marched right out the door. I should have been offended. I had every right to be pissed off at how she'd spoken to me when I'd been nothing but nice. But there was something about her, something I couldn't put my finger on, that told me I wasn't getting to see the real Adalyn.

She had put on a good front, but there was something hidden in her eyes that gave her away. Maybe tonight I'd get a chance to find out what that was.

CHAPTER 5

ADALYN

"What the hell, Adalyn? Why did you treat him like he was dog shit stuck to the bottom of your shoe? That was really embarrassing. I have spent weeks telling him great things about you and trying to get you this job and you undid everything in 2.5 seconds by turning into the world's biggest bitch."

Finally relaxing my shoulders and back muscles now that we were out of the building, my body ached from the strain. I didn't realize how badly I had tensed up during our little altercation.

Why *did* I react like that?

Hell, I knew why. But no sane person would understand, so why bother explaining? That smile. That smile made me shiver all the way to my toes. It made me simultaneously feel a mix of lust and hatred. Not that he's ever done anything to cause me to hate him, but I've seen that smile before. The one that all the charming, egotistical assholes use to manipulate women.

His smile did seem somewhat genuine, but I knew better. I'm not an idiot. He may not have been pretending because he was being malicious, but it still wasn't real. Most likely it was for Stacy's benefit. If not for her, he never would have given me a second glance. If his fancy suit and expensive haircut were any indication, he most likely dated models or dimwitted socialites. So why waste my time with someone who was only being nice for someone else's benefit? I didn't accept charity from anyone, even when it came to friendships. I didn't have many friends and there was a reason for that. I guarded myself closely.

"I'm sorry Stacy. I'm just in a mood and I was caught off guard. I didn't know I was going to be meeting a potential future boss today. Not to mention one that is hot enough to melt the sun. You could have given me a heads up, you know. Look at me, I'm a mess. How the hell do you know him anyway? You've never mentioned him."

"Since when does dressing to impress matter to you? You and I both know you would have done nothing different if you had known. If anything, you would have intentionally made yourself look ridiculous, you crazy bitch. And he is Carrie's older brother, so I've known him as long as I've known her and he's really not a bad guy. Even despite all of his money and success, he's pretty down to earth."

"Yeah, because a two-thousand-dollar suit is so down to earth. Maybe you just don't see it because you've known him so long or something, but he's no different than any other cocky prick."

"You're wrong, Adalyn," Stacy snapped at me. I

jerked my head back in surprise at the anger in her voice. "You shouldn't make so many assumptions about people. I know you have a history with guys like that and I'm sure your opinion of Carrie might affect your view of him as well, but Ian is *not* like that. If you gave him half a chance you would see that."

"You're right, that was seriously shitty of me," I sighed, my shoulders sinking as the guilt took over. "You know how I am; I push people away. I sabotage good opportunities. And honestly, he was just so fucking hot that I panicked."

"Well, you should apologize. Carrie can be difficult to get along with, but Ian's never met an enemy. Well, once, but he's seriously the easiest guy to get along with and his employees love him."

She knew what she was asking of me. Apologizing did not come easily for me, especially when it came to men. But Stacy was right. I had judged him before I got to know him and he was obviously important to her, so tonight I would have to suck it up and make the effort.

I'd always been this way - ruining any chance of happiness. It had gotten worse over the years. It wasn't until I started therapy after the incident that I realized what I was doing and why. My therapist said I intentionally did the opposite of what others expected of me as a way of pushing them away so I didn't have to face rejection.

If that's not a slap in the face, I don't know what is. I've got insecurities just like the next person, but I'm not so hard on myself that I just assume everyone is going to immediately dislike me. The more I thought about it though, the more it made sense. People are users. They take what they can from you until you have nothing left to give, then they move on. So I stopped wasting my time long ago and quit trying to please the people around me and started living for myself.

It only strengthened my determination to ruin my own chances at happiness when I found that I could truly relate to someone or see myself enjoying spending any amount of time with them. I would start intentionally saying things I knew would offend them, or would behave obnoxiously. Anything I could do to make them not want to be around me.

Very few had seen right through my efforts and made their way into my heart. Stacy was one of them. She saw right through my bullshit and called me on it constantly. Every time she did, it ended in a fight. We would scream at each other for about an hour and then curl up on the couch and watch a movie, eating ice cream, as if nothing had even happened. We were bat shit crazy like that. Fight hard, love hard. That was our motto since we met freshman year.

Pulling myself out of my daze, I looked at a very impatient Stacy staring at me like she was trying to set fire to my hair through telepathy.

"Ok fine, slut. Let's go find me a dress. To make it up to you, I'll even let you pick out my shoes and jewelry."

Stacy squealed and slipped her arm through mine, linking us at the elbows. She returned my glare with a knowing smirk. She was in my personal space. I did not like to be touched, but she didn't care. Making me uncomfortable was one of her favorite pastimes.

"Chop, chop clit breath. Bitches gotta get shit done."

Chapter 6

Adalyn

"I changed my mind, Stacy. I can't wear this." I felt like my vagina was waving at me in the mirror. I swear this dress wasn't this short when I tried it on earlier. Did I buy the wrong size? Did I gain fifteen pounds in the last three hours? What the hell.

"Ughhhhhh. Are you trying to get me thrown in jail? Because I will seriously fuck you up if you don't stop whining. If busting up your face is the only way to shut you up, then I'll do it. Don't test me."

"I hate you."

"No, you love me. Now get your shoes on and let's go. My vagina is getting really antsy and is ready for some entertaining, and that can't happen if I stay here listening to your annoying crap. Unless you grew a penis overnight and didn't tell me."

"I really think you should join a sex addicts anonymous group, Stacy. Actually, you know what, never mind. You'd end up just using it as a way to meet people to sleep with. The whole thing would probably turn into an orgy."

"See, that's why I love you so much, hooker. You know me so well. That's actually not a half bad idea, either. Although, I think the issue here is that YOU are the one who needs to get laid."

"Um, no. I'm so scarred from that last guy; I may stay celibate for the rest of my life."

"Was he the 'farter' or the squeaker?"

"Oh, God...the 'farter'." Ugh, that night was traumatic. "I totally forgot about him. He had no shame. Who farts every time they thrust into you and doesn't even try to act embarrassed or apologize for it? I almost threw up on him. Then the idiot had the balls to ask me out on a second date before he left. That really was a low point in my sex life."

"That's not nearly as bad as the guy who slapped me across the face right when he came. I had a fucking bruise on my face for a week! Apparently bitch slapping me during his climax was okay but me kneeing him in the balls was "crossing the line,"" she said that last part using her fingers to make air quotes.

I was rolling around on the ground, clutching my stomach and trying to catch my breath. I was laughing so hard it felt like I'd had the wind knocked out of me. Tears were streaming down my face. It's sad how many of these stories we had. My dress was going to get all wrinkled and my ass was probably flashing her, but I was laughing too hard to care.

"And no, the squeaker was like three mistakes ago." I sat up trying to catch my breath, feeling winded from laughing for so long. "Where did we find these guys? I

seriously felt like I was being pounded by a rubber duck."
Of all the nights I wished I drank alcohol so I could just
black out the memories, that was definitely one of them.

"Oh my god!" Stacy yelled, doubling over with
laughter. "Is he the guy you made donkey sounds with?"

"Yep. Apparently he thought his sounding like a
chew toy was hot, but when I would 'hee-haw' it made
me "just fucking weird." Men… such double standards."

"Whatever, nothing is as bad as the titty slapper."
Stacy could always one up me when it came to embarrassing sex stories. Even with my competitiveness, I was
more than happy to lose with this one. "My girls had
never seen such abuse. I like a good spanking as much
as the next girl, but smacking my tits over and over is
not hot."

"Alright, you win, Stace. If we keep going, we'll
be here all night reminiscing over our biggest mistakes."

"True. Lord knows I've got plenty of them. Let's
get out of here before you change your mind, slut bag."

Ten minutes and thirty dollars in cab fare later, we
arrived at the club. Grind, aka, my personal hell for the
night. On top of all of the other reasons I didn't want to
be here, now I had to apologize to Ian. That alone made
me want to vomit. I felt like my legs weighed a thousand
pounds each. Physically exiting the cab and walking up

to the building took every ounce of energy I had. There used to be a time when I would be excited to be getting VIP treatment at an exclusive club. That time was not now. That time felt like a hundred years ago.

As soon as the bouncer opened the door for us, I was smacked in the face with a wall of loud music and heat. I had to admit, it was a really nice club. A live band was playing to the far right on a corner stage. There was a second level that wrapped around the entire perimeter of the club, overlooking the packed dance floor. Several high top tables were spread out sporadically around the large room.

Stacy immediately spotted Carrie and grabbed my hand, dragging me behind her. Instinctively I resisted, not wanting to talk to Carrie, and when my hand slipped from hers I stumbled at the loss of contact and started to face plant right into the ground. I pinballed off a couple of people on the dance floor, but just as I was about to go down, large hands wrapped around my waist, saving me from my demise.

I found my balance and turned around to thank whoever was kind enough to prevent me from going home with a concussion before the night even started, but I almost fell again from the shock of looking directly into the face of Ian. He was wearing that same shit eating grin as he was earlier. Rat bastard.

Roughly shoving his hands off my body, I said

thank you and turned to walk away. He grabbed my hand though, preventing my escape. I hated him in that moment. Maybe that wasn't fair, considering it was really my own body that was pissing me off. Were my nipples seriously getting hard from him grabbing my hand? Maybe Stacy was right, I really did need to get laid. My inability to control my body's reaction to him made me more furious than ever. Why did he have to be so damn hot?

Determined not to let him get to me, I went to yank my hand from his grasp and almost fell backwards. *Why do I keep almost falling!?* He let go easier than I expected and a flash of relief, and then disappointment, ran through me.

Disappointment? What the hell, Addy. Get your crap together. He is the enemy. Your nipples are not hard; you are not aching with need. You are just mad. You are not thinking about hot, angry sex with this man. Not at all. Well, maybe just a little….

Before I could recover from almost falling again and the argument I was currently having with myself over whether or not one hot, steamy night with Ian would be acceptable, he wrapped his hand around my waist again and gripped my neck, pulling my face to his. I felt his breath warm on my ear. *Damn it all to hell, I just shivered.* Considering I was already a little sweaty from the heat coming off all of the writhing bodies on the dance floor, he most definitely knew that I did not shiver from being cold. Nope. Now he knew I was attracted to him. Shit on a pretzel stick.

"You put on a good show, but I know you feel it, sunshine. Your body craves mine as much as mine craves yours. You might mask your desire as hostility, but I see right through your bullshit. I will break through those barriers of yours, I can promise you that. I won't give up until you are writhing underneath my body, spread out on my bed, screaming my name in pleasure."

Cocky prick. Sexy as hell cocky prick. Fighting to maintain control of myself and resisting the urge to slip out my tongue and lick his neck, I shoved him as hard as I could and he actually stumbled for a second, clearly caught off guard by my reaction. What did he think? That he could just whisper some bullshit nonsense in my ear and I would just fall to his feet? Yeah, my panties were soaking wet and my knees were weak, but like hell was I going to give him the satisfaction of knowing that.

Turning and managing to escape this time, I made my way toward the bar, scanning the crowd unsuccessfully for Stacy. Spotting an empty stool at the bar, I sat down and motioned for the bartender. My nerves were frazzled and an impulsive need to calm down took over, easily pushing aside all of the rational parts of my brain telling me that alcohol wasn't the answer. This man got under my skin like no one I had ever met before. Most guys would have called me a bitch or an assortment of colorful names by now and given up. Why was he trying so hard to mess with me? He clearly could have any woman he wanted, yet he felt the need to piss me off with his over the top flirting.

When the bartender made his way over to me I realized I had no idea what to order. He was tall and muscular, with shaggy blonde hair. His white t-shirt clung to him like it was a second skin and you could actually see his abs through it. He was hot and he was grinning at me, his head tilted to the left, patiently waiting for my order despite the numerous hands waving for him to come refill their drinks. Under normal circumstances, this type of attention from such an attractive man would have made me uncomfortable, but already being shaken up from feeling Ian's breath on my neck while his body pressed into mine, had me verging on the edge of numbness.

Right when I started to open my mouth, Ian stepped up next to me, putting his hand on my lower back. The club was so packed that he had to wedge his way in between myself and another woman, who was so beautiful it physically hurt me to be sitting next to her. She tried to smile at him, but he didn't even notice. Instead he pressed himself up against my side, not even trying to pretend that he wasn't intentionally pushing his hard cock against my leg, and I cursed myself for liking it.

My legs immediately clenched, trying to slow the pulsing between my thighs. *Ugh, I'm so weak*. Stiffening my spine, I closed my eyes and counted to 10. If I didn't calm down I was either going to kiss him or smack him. Both sounded highly enjoyable. Maybe I could kiss him *then* smack him. *No. No kissing Adalyn.*

Ian ordered something from the bartender. I had no idea what it was. I couldn't hear over all the blood pounding in my ears while I glared at his smug face. *Control yourself, Addy. Don't let him know he's getting to you. No reaction, feign indifference.*

"Drinks are on me, Sunshine. What would you like?"

"I don't drink. The only thing I would like right now is for you to get your hands off of me and take a hint. Oh, and stop calling me Sunshine."

"You afraid to let your guard down around me? Don't worry, I wouldn't take advantage of you if you were drunk. I want to make sure that when I finally get you in my bed you remember every little detail."

"No, I just don't usually drink. But you should know that if you're trying to get me to go home with you then I would most definitely need to be completely shit-faced before I would ever willingly get in your car. So if getting me naked is your end goal then you might have to rethink that whole 'not taking advantage of me when I'm drunk' thing."

He looked at me incredulously. Was it because I said I didn't drink or that I wouldn't go home with him? Probably the drinking thing, it was a pretty common reaction. Why was it so bizarre that I didn't drink? Everyone looked at me like I was insane every time I said that, and they always wanted to know why. It was a conversation I would never have, so asking was a waste of time. Normally I would try to deflect or change the subject, but if that didn't work I'd just say I was a recovering alcoholic. I didn't care what people thought, I just didn't want to talk about it.

"Aw, is princess afraid of losing control? Are you so uptight that you can't let yourself have even a small amount of fun? Must be hard walking around with that giant stick up your ass all the time. Probably for the best. Wouldn't want you to let your guard down and end up doing something crazy, like being nice for once."

Ass.

The bartender returned with Ian's drink and I leaned forward, fisting a handful of the bartender's shirt and leaned in to speak into his ear.

"Bring me 4 shots of whatever is the strongest you've got."

When I let go, he winked at me and I giggled before he walked away. Intentionally giggled, of course. No self respecting woman actually giggles. Glancing at Ian out of the corner of my eye, I could see the shock in his face. And for the first time, anger. Aha! Finally. So that's how to make this asshole angry. Bruise his ego. Heaven forbid there be one woman on earth who doesn't throw themselves at him.

"I have no problem with having fun or being crazy, I just choose not to do either of those things with *you*."

He winced and actually looked genuinely hurt by my comment and I immediately felt guilty. I was supposed to be apologizing to him and trying harder for Stacy. But something about him just got me so worked up and it was like I literally couldn't help myself.

"I'm sorry. I was a bitch to you earlier and I'm still doing it now, and I promised Stacy I would try harder to get along with you. So... I'm sorry."

"What was that?" He asked with a huge grin, leaning his ear closer to my mouth. "I knew eventually my charm and dashing good looks would get to you."

"Ha! Keep telling yourself that. I'm just being nice for Stacy's sake."

"You know I don't really believe that, right? You think I don't see, and feel, the way your body reacts to mine? If it's the chase you want, if you want me to work for it, then I will. But there's no denying that there's something between us, Adalyn."

That kind of cocky attitude is exactly what pissed me off about him. I guess I should thank him for reminding me of that. Hating him was a lot easier than pretending to get along.

The bartender returned with my shots and lined them up in front of me. I shyly smiled at him before yanking on his shirt and pulling his mouth to mine. We shared a brief, albeit wonderfully sexy, kiss. When I pulled away he winked again and turned to take another order. I don't know where the urge to do that even came from. Okay, that's a lie. I wanted to show Ian I could be impulsive, and if it made him jealous, then that was just a perk.

Wait. *Jealous?* Why did I care if he was jealous?

No time to explore that thought. Without looking at Ian, I immediately downed all 4 shots, one right after the other. Dammit, they burned. And were disgusting. I fought the urge to gag or let it show on my face just how much I had not enjoyed those shots.

Once I got my now churning stomach under control, I turned to face Ian. Now I was the one with the smug face. I'm not sure why, though. That was probably one of the dumbest things I had ever done. What was I thinking? I wasn't. I wasn't thinking. I was pissed and he challenged me and my obsessive need to always win an argument made me want to prove a point. And based on his knowing smile, that's exactly what he had wanted. I fell right into his trap. SHIT.

I needed to find Stacy. Fast. I needed someone to know what I'd just done before the alcohol took over. I wasn't experienced with this, but considering I never drank and I'd asked for something strong, I assumed I was about to be falling down drunk in a very short amount of time. If the warmth spreading through my extremities was anything to go by, I was already halfway there.

After spinning in circles a few times, I finally spotted her. Whoa, spinning was a bad idea. She reached me just as I started to wobble. I could see the confusion in her face, though she was starting to look a bit blurry.

"What is wrong with you, Addy? Are you okay?"

I tried to explain, but apparently my reactions were already delayed from the alcohol and I took too long to speak up.

"She just tossed back 4 shots."

I tried to turn to glare at Ian who was close behind me, but my eyelids felt heavy and I wasn't sure if I was glaring or looked like I had fallen asleep midair. Stupid Ian. This was all his fault. With his stupid gorgeous body, wrapped tight in those dark denim jeans and a plain black t-shirt that looked like it had been painted on. With his stupid beautiful eyes that made me want to reveal all my secret desires and beg him to take me to bed. With his stupid face that I wanted to lick as if he were a delicious ice cream cone. *Why do I keep thinking about licking him?* Fighting the urge to act out my irrational thoughts was proving to be a lot more difficult in my inebriated state.

Keep tongue in mouth. Keep tongue in mouth. Tongue. In his mouth. My tongue in his mouth. DAMMIT.

"Dammit, Ian. Why did you let her do this? She never drinks. She's going to be completely wasted. She is going to be so pissed tomorrow. And you better believe I will not take the fall for this shit. When she's hungover and looking for someone to blame I will gladly be throwing you under the bus." Stacy wrapped her arm around me and led me to a couch. "Can you sit with her for a minute while I get a bottle of water? And can you manage to not let her do any more stupid shit until I get back?" Then Stacy was gone, leaving me in the hands of someone I felt the growing need to be far, far away from. I could feel him smiling at me.

Dick.

Mmm, I wonder if he has a big dick. STOP IT. He *is* a dick. Don't think about his *actual* dick. And quit thinking the word dick!

I could feel Ian chuckling as he sat entirely too close to me on the couch. Why is he laughing? Did I just say all that out loud? Ugh, I couldn't even tell if I was thinking things or actually saying them. I was so screwed. His enjoyment from this was making me so angry I could have punched kittens. *Someone find me a kitten to punch!*

"What, you couldn't get any closer? Why don't you just sit on my fucking lap?" Did I really just ask him that? I sounded hateful, but I wasn't sure my body was backing up my words. I couldn't even bring myself to look at him, but I saw a finger trailing down his chest. *Who the hell is touching him right now?* Oh my God, that's MY finger. Why couldn't I stop my hand from moving? *Help! Someone! Mayday! Mayday!*

Obviously, I no longer had control over any part of my body. All I could do at that point was pray that I would black out and not be able to remember any details when I woke up tomorrow. I'd take having my head in a toilet in the morning over having to relive these humiliating memories any day.

Ian grabbed my finger and pulled it to his mouth, kissing the tip. *There I go shivering again.* Maybe I was just getting the flu. *Sure, Addy, keep lying to yourself.* Dammit! Now my own brain was making me mad! *Hey brain, shut up! No one asked you!*

His face was so close to mine. If I moved just an inch towards him our lips would be touching. He was looking at me like…I had no idea what that look was on his face. Somewhere deep inside I knew that whatever that expression was, it would normally piss me off. Right then, thanks to the alcohol, it was making me feel warm and tingly all over. I wanted him to kiss my finger again. I wanted him to kiss all my fingers. Then my lips. Then maybe he would kiss my jaw, down my neck, trailing down between my breasts.

Get it together, Adalyn. Snap out of it.

Stacy returned just in time to save me from doing something I would undoubtedly regret tomorrow. I chugged the bottle of water, feeling some of it drip down my chin and land on my chest. I looked over to see Ian staring at that drop of water like we were in the middle of the Sahara and he was dying of thirst. I could see his chest rising and falling heavily and his pulse pick up tempo on his neck. Mmmmmm...his neck.

I couldn't tell if it was the water dribbling out of my mouth or if I was actually drooling over him again, but I was interrupted by a group of guys who came barreling towards us before I had the chance to figure it out.

One of them immediately snatched Stacy up by her waist and pulled her off the floor and into a big bear hug. She giggled as he placed her back down, then made his way over to Ian. Ian stood and did one of those secret bro shakes that all typical man children do. The other two guys were talking to Stacy, but then bro shake guy turned to me.

"Hey, you're Adalyn."

"No shit. Gold star to bro shake for stating the obvious," I said rolling my eyes.

He chuckled at me and shook his head. He looked relaxed with an easy smile. I immediately liked him. He was attractive, but not really my type. A little on the thin side with tattoos up his arms and a piercing in his lower lip. The fact that I wasn't sexually attracted to him made it a lot easier for me to tame my inner bitch a little.

"I'm Brett, Stacy's friend. Stacy says you're an amazing singer, and here in about 20 minutes we're going to start doing some live karaoke. Was hoping I could talk you into joining us up on stage. It being the first night, not sure if a whole lot of people are going to be up to participating. Trying to recruit some people ahead of time."

Normally I would have given a snarky, self-deprecating response, but Ian beat me to it.

"Sorry, Brett. Think you're fighting a losing battle with this one. No way will you be able to get Sunshine to lower her inhibitions enough to get up there. Her idea of fun is making everyone around her miserable."

I could tell by the wink Ian gave me that he was just trying to tease me, but I knew better than anyone that even jokes have some meaning behind them. He might have been making light of the situation, but he obviously thought I was just a stone cold bitch who had no idea how to have fun.

"I'll get up there and sing a song with you on one condition, Brett."

"You name it, babe."

Pulling Brett close to me, I told him my condition. I was regretting the words as they were coming out, but I didn't back down from a challenge, so whether or not I would regret it later, I was going through with it. I wasn't oblivious to the fact that the alcohol that still remained in my system was probably a big factor in my willingness to get up in front of a couple thousand people and potentially make an ass out of myself.

When I pulled away, Brett returned my wide grin with one of his own, reaching out his hand to shake on our little agreement. Ian's eyebrows were raised, showing his surprise, but he wasn't surprised enough. What would it take for me to really throw this guy off his game?

Well, game on Ian, I thought as I tossed back another shot and grabbed Brett's hand, making my way towards the stage. Game. On.

CHAPTER 7

IAN

This was by far the most fun I'd had in a long time. Getting under this girl's skin had quickly become my new addiction in life. The way her face flushed with red, her eyebrows knit together and her nose scrunched. It was much more subtle when she was sober and a lot more ridiculous with alcohol in her, but it was adorable either way.

It was almost too easy. Almost. Maybe I just knew all the right triggers to really piss her off. I had a feeling there was a lot more to her than I realized, and now more than ever I was determined to figure out what made this girl tick.

I could have sworn I was having a heart attack when I first spotted her tonight as I walked in the club. I literally could feel my heart constrict and then slow until it felt like it just stopped. She was wearing a tight black dress that stopped several inches above her knee. It was a halter top, cut low enough to show plenty of cleavage from her, what I would guess, around D cup size chest. Her hair was in loose waves and she had a smoky look to her eyes. Those ridiculously high heels did wonders for her legs. Legs that I wanted wrapped around my face.

Edging my way closer to the stage, I could see the

other men staring at her. Some were catcalling and whis-
tling. I felt an unexpected and fierce possessiveness over
her. I had the urge to yank her off the stage and carry her
out the door and to the safety of my car where I wouldn't
have to share her with any other men's leering glances.
If I thought for half a second that she would actually let
me do that without making a scene or clawing my eyes
out, then I would. Baby steps.

Brett said something into the microphone while the
band set back up. I couldn't hear him, mostly because I
wasn't really paying attention. I couldn't take my eyes
off of her. She was less drunk, the immediate effects of
the alcohol starting to wear off, but she was so relaxed.
She was laughing at something Brett whispered in her
ear and she looked so happy. I wanted to be the one making her laugh and seeing that happiness in her eyes.

One day. One day I would be on the receiving end
of that smile.

The drums started, snapping me out of my daze, and
then my heart really did stop. Her voice wrapped itself
around me, gripping me so tight I felt like I couldn't get
a breath. I couldn't even tell you what she was singing.
Everything but her faded out. The people, the sounds, the
lights, the smells. It was like they had put a spotlight on
her and everything else disappeared.

I should be scolding myself for thinking like such
a pussy, but I couldn't bring myself to care. She was

enchanting. Mesmerizing. Maybe once she got off the stage she could give me my balls back, because she was clearly in charge of them now.

I snapped myself out of my trance when the song ended, but they immediately started into another one. I recognized it right away but didn't know what song it was. Wait…is that…The Humpty Hump? I couldn't help myself. I doubled over with laughter. She caught me, but instead of being mad for laughing like I thought she might be, she winked at me.

This playful side of her was almost too much. Sexy, feisty, and funny. That was a dangerous combo. I wanted to pull her to me and kiss her. Hard. If I could handle the rejection, I'd do it anyway, but I was too lost in her right now to be able to pretend her obvious disdain for me didn't hurt my ego as badly as it did.

I didn't mind working for a relationship. Putting in the effort, the romantic gestures, all of the crap my buddies pretended to be too macho to do for a woman. I just hadn't found the right one. Well, I thought I had. But I didn't make mistakes twice. I needed to get to know Adalyn. I needed to know if my instincts about her were right. There once was a day when I'd never doubt my own instincts. I'd learned my lesson though, and I was going to be more cautious this time.

CHAPTER 8

ADALYN

Holy shit. Shit. I just did that. I just sang on stage. In front of hundreds of people. I'm a fucking rock star.

"Yeah you are, slut!" Stacy yelled as I walked off stage.

"Shit, did I say that out loud? Ugh, my filter is even worse than normal. Please take me home before I do anything else I'll regret."

"You are so not going to regret that tomorrow. I got it recorded on my phone and we are going to watch that bad ass shit when you're sober so you can appreciate it. I am so proud of you. You were amazing."

Grabbing and downing two of the celebratory shots Stacy had ordered in honor of my performance, I realized I was way past the point of making sound decisions. After pouring my heart out into some Britney pop shit, I immediately felt embarrassed. What's the cure for embarrassment? Laughter. I had anticipated feeling this way after actually trying and singing a song out of my comfort zone, so I told Brett that we had to immediately go into The Humpty Hump. It worked like a charm and had the desired effect. People were laughing and having such a good time that by the end of the second song, my first one was long forgotten. This ensured that even if I sucked, it didn't matter.

"Shut up before I vomit on your shoes. I'm gonna quit while I'm ahead and get out of here. You can stay if you want, I'm just gonna grab my purse."

"No way, dickbreath, I'm coming with you. You're so shit faced you'd probably pass out in the back of the cab and the cabbie would have to drag your drunk ass up to our door and I am not cleaning your puke up off our porch."

I tried to slap Stacy but I didn't even come close to hitting her, and the momentum of it knocked us into a group of people standing off to the side. Stacy and I were giggling and apologizing, but whoever I had bumped into was apparently very unhappy.

"You idiot!" Carrie yelled, pushing my shoulder with her hand, knocking me back a couple steps. "You just made me spill my drink all over my dress! What is wrong with you!"

"Calm down, Carrie, it was an accident," Stacy tried to assure her, but I wasn't sure Carrie even heard her because her eyes continued to burn holes into mine. I started to speak up and apologize but Carrie huffed off before I had a chance. Stacy and I just looked at each other and fell into a fit of laughter. We had a tendency to giggle uncontrollably in tense situations.

"Wait, let me grab my purse," I told Stacy as I pulled her towards the couch I'd been occupying before my vocal debut.

"Shit! Where is it?! Where is my fucking purse!?" I was looking around frantically, even dropped to my knees on the disgusting floor to look on the floor under the couch.

"Okay, first off, you have to stand up. Apparently your purse isn't the only thing you lost. Where the hell are your panties?"

"What? Oh. This dress was too tight; I didn't want a panty line. I wasn't anticipating crawling around on the floor. Oops." Flashing my lady parts was the least of my worries if I couldn't find my purse. "I just ran up on the stage and left it here on the couch without thinking. It had my phone and everything in it. DAMMIT." Turning to see Ian approaching, I growled. "YOU! This is all YOUR fault!"

Throwing up his hands in a gesture of innocence he came to a stop.

"I was all the way across the room. How could I have possibly pissed you off now?"

"My purse was stolen because of you!"

"Yeah, okay, I still don't see how I have anything to do with your purse getting stolen."

"You…you distracted me. You are always distracting me. You…ugh…you are so frustrating!"

Spinning in circles, trying to process what to do, I swayed to the left bumping into Ian. *I have* got *to stop spinning.* Spinning and shots equaled Ian's arms around my waist and my guard was down low enough for me to feel my desire dripping down my leg just from his touch. Dammit, where are panties when you need them.

Suddenly, with the combination of the alcohol and stress from losing my purse, my body decided it was nap time. Never mind the fact that I was standing in the middle of a packed club. Nope. That didn't matter. My legs just decided they were done for the night, and down I went.

Ian, always jumping to my rescue, wrapped his arms around me yet again. Instead of pushing away from him like my brain was telling me to do, my body decided snuggling was a better option. *C'mon, brain. Get control of the situation here.* Okay... my brain was giving my brain a pep talk to control my body. I'd officially lost it. But he was so warm and my body fit perfectly into his side. Being in his arms just felt right, and while normally that would freak me out, I was too tired and too drunk to fight it. Goodbye rational thought, hello bad decisions.

"I'm so sad, Ian. I lost my phone and my pretty pink sparkly purse with my favorite lip gloss and my Starbucks gift card. How will I get coffee now? My lips will be dull and dry and I'll be too tired to care that I can't call anyone because I'll be caffeine deprived. Why is life so cruel?"

Aaaand...kill me now. No really. I'd rather be dead

than be living through this.

I could feel him chuckling as he squeezed me tighter. It felt familiar, his hold around me. I didn't know why. I hated being touched. I couldn't remember the last time I let a man hold me like that without pushing him away or cringing. No matter the reasons for why I felt so comfortable right then, all I could do was let out a heavy sigh and relax further into his hard body.

I wanted to dip my hand into his shirt. I wanted to rub my fingertips all over his hard chest, tracing down his abs, down to his glorious abdomen that led directly to his happy place. *Happy place?* I really was gone.

Holy hell, I was actually trying to put my hand in his shirt. What's worse is that I couldn't stop. Thankfully he had the good sense to do it for me. Giving my hand a light squeeze and smiling down at me, he started towards the exit.

"Come on, sunshine. Let's get some fresh air and you can use my phone to call the police. We'll get this figured out for you. You can feel me up all you want once we get you sobered up."

"Why are you being so nice to me? I'm such a bitch to you. You make me so angry. I can't help it. Why do you make me so angry? I want to touch your face."

Laughing and moving my hand from his face, he continued to hold me gingerly. Like I was made of porcelain. That should have made me angry. I was not weak;

I didn't need to be babied. But he was so warm and cozy, I just couldn't muster up the energy to be mad.

"I'm being nice to you because you are drunk and need someone to take care of you, and despite whatever it is you think of me, I'm actually a pretty decent guy. At least, I like to think I am. And I make you angry because I can. You make it so easy, and you are so adorable when you get frustrated I just can't help myself."

"You think I'm adorable?"

"Among other things."

"What other things?"

"Maybe we should have this conversation when you are sober."

"I think you know me well enough by now to know that this conversation will never happen when I'm sober. And since I plan on never drinking again, this is your one chance to take advantage of my vulnerable self." I immediately came to a halt and stiffened from my own words. He didn't let me stop for long though, instead he urged me to keep going.

When we finally emerged from the club, the cold air felt amazing against my hot skin. I didn't know if I was hot from the club or from the beautiful man's arms wrapped around me, but either way I was on fire. My skin was slick with sweat and was covered in goose bumps from the cold. Ever the gentleman, Ian draped a jacket over my shoulders. Where did he even get a jacket? Damn him. He was making it harder and harder to hate him.

Stacy stepped out moments after we did, and Ian walked us both over to the side of the club and told us to lean against the wall and not move while he called the police.

"Bossy bastard."

Stacy and I burst out into an uncontrollable fit of giggles, and strangers turned and stared. I'm sure we were a sight. Sweaty, disheveled, drunk and giggling. Slinking down to the ground Stacy and I laid our heads back, legs stretched out, crossed at the ankle. Despite how badly the evening had started, I was actually having a lot of fun. Probably the most fun I'd had in a really long time.

"I think Ian's into you."

Snorting derisively at Stacy's remark, I couldn't help but inwardly feel the butterflies of longing. I was still too drunk to stop them before it happened. Longing is not something I allowed myself to feel. Still, I couldn't help but let my mind wander for just a moment and imagine what it would be like to actually go on a date with Ian. Would he take me to a nice restaurant? Show up at my doorstep with flowers? Treat me to a romantic evening? I would hate all of those things. Something told me he would know that, though. He read me so well it scared me.

It didn't matter. I couldn't entertain those types of thoughts. Ian dated the city's elite, not boring, simple girls like me. I could never give him what he wanted. He was used to the nice restaurants and romantic evenings. It's what normal girls expected and enjoyed. If he really was the nice guy I was starting to believe he was, then he deserved better than me anyway. I still didn't even know what he did for a living, but it was obvious he had lots of money. I was sure he wouldn't want my baggage coming along and screwing up his perfect life.

Just as my thoughts took a depressing turn, my pity party was halted by the approaching cop car. An extremely attractive man stepped out from the driver's side and Stacy and I simultaneously went slack jawed. Damn, he wore that uniform well. He was the verify definition of tall, dark and handsome. My thoughts were too preoccupied with Ian currently to be affected by this man's good looks, but Stacy was always a sucker for a man in uniform.

Looking over at her confirmed my suspicions. This was about to get interesting. If the sparkle in her eye and devious grin she was wearing wasn't enough to convince me that she was about to do something stupid, then her not-so-casually yanking the top of her dress down to expose more cleavage was a dead giveaway.

Ian immediately shook the officer's hand, explaining the situation. It was a miracle there was someone sober and responsible there to help us. I didn't think I could form a coherent sentence right then. The fact that Ian kept having to take care of me sobered me up just a little, though.

The officer eyed us speculatively, obviously assessing our drunken state. I'm sure we were a hot mess. We were still in a hysterical state of laughter when the officer approached.

"Good evening, ladies. I'm Officer Chad Stevens. I am here to…"

Before he could even finish his sentence, Stacy was trying to stand. Trying being the key word there. When she finally made it to her feet, she immediately put her hands on the officer's chest and tried to give him a seductive look but ended up looking more like she was constipated.

"Hey, Officer Sexy Pants. Are you here to arrest me for being a very, very bad girl? You might want to use your cuffs, I can be very feisty," she slurred, her face inches from his.

The officer took her hands and gently pushed them away and looked at her with a mix of pity and annoyance. Did this happen to him often? Even drunk I'd imagine not very many women would have the balls to be so forward with a cop the way she was. I'd always envied her confidence when it came to men. Not right at that moment, though. Right then I was too busy laughing at her to be jealous of anything.

"Ma'am, unless you've committed an actual crime then no, I am not here to arrest you. However, you ladies have clearly had a lot to drink tonight, so I hope neither of you had planned on getting behind the wheel."

"No sir," Ian chimed in. "I'll make sure they get home safely. They took a cab here."

Stacy, being the idiotic slut she was, decided it would be a good time to try and solicit a man coming out of the club, offering her services in exchange for money. What the hell was she doing? She was being so ridiculous and normally I would be mortified, but I was too drunk to care. I dug Stacy's phone out of her purse and tried to take a video, but I was too inebriated to figure out how to unlock the damn screen.

"Excuse me, ma'am. I don't know what you think you're doing, but you can't solicit a man for sex, especially in front of an officer. Are you *trying* to get arrested?" All pity was gone from the officer's face and all that remained was the annoyance.

"Why yes, officer. I think you'll quickly realize just how determined I am. If breaking the law is what I need to do to get you to put your hands on me, then that's what I'll do. I'll even resist a little. I like it rough."

Oh good God, Stacy, shut up.

The officer grabbed Stacy's elbow and lead her towards his car. You could see the excitement in her eyes.

She clearly thought she'd gotten to him, but apparently she was too drunk to see what was really on his face. Anger. He was not amused by her antics. He gently pushed her into the back of his car, but when she smiled and started to speak, he slammed the door in her face. Stacy started banging on the window, calling the officer all sorts of colorful names. With his back to her and her shouts muffled behind the window, you could see the smirk he was trying to conceal. He was enjoying making Stacy angry.

"I think this one needs a night in lock up to teach her how to behave in public. Will you make sure your friend gets home safely and tell her to report to the station in the morning when she has sobered up to give a report?" Ian politely nodded, but the look on his face made a bubble of laughter burst from my mouth when he finally registered what the officer had just said.

"You're not actually going to file charges against her, are you?" Ian looked shocked, but quickly relaxed when the officer laughed and gestured dismissively to his question.

"No, I won't document anything. Just want to scare some sense into her. As soon as she sobers up enough to make it home, I'll let her go." Ian hurriedly handed the officer Stacy's purse. "Have a nice night," the officer said to us as he got in his car.

And as quickly as he came, the officer left, and I

was alone in the hands of my new pseudo enemy. That fine line between love and hate? I was walking it right then. And I was scared shitless at which way I was going to fall.

CHAPTER 9

IAN

I could see Adalyn's struggle to gain control over her mind. She had a look on her face of intense concentration, her eyebrows scrunched together and a scowl on her face. Getting her in my car had been quite a struggle. Even when she could barely walk she still put up a good fight. That flirty, cute Adalyn that had walked out of the club with me was long gone. Cold and closed off Adalyn had returned yet again.

"Quit looking at me and keep your eyes on the road, dumbass. I'd like to make it back to my apartment alive. I may not have a job, a boyfriend or any idea what to do with my life, but I still *have* a life and I'd like to keep it that way."

She was hunched over, arms crossed, looking straight ahead. It was adorable. I bit the inside of my cheek to try and keep from smirking but it didn't work and when she caught me smiling she became even more agitated.

"I'm glad you're enjoying yourself. Laugh it up, buddy, because this is the last time I'll ever let myself be in the position to take any kind of help from you. I don't need a knight in shining armor, so quit trying to weasel your way into my life. I don't know what kind of game

you're playing, but I'm not going to give in to your ma-
nipulations. Save it for one of your floozies who are too
dumb to see through your bullshit."

"Okay, I don't even know where to begin with what
you just said. First of all, I wasn't laughing, I was smiling. It's not my fault everything you do makes me smile,
even when you're being a giant pain in my ass. Second of
all, what game do you think I'm playing? I'm not trying
to weasel my way into anything and I can certainly tell
you don't need saving. Why does my wanting to spend
time with you have to have an ulterior motive? And lastly, why do you assume all the women I date are dumb?
That's pretty judgmental of you. Although, based on the
assumptions you've obviously already made about me,
I should have deduced just how judgmental you could
be."

She visibly winced and I could see the guilt on her
face. Finally, some real progress. This facade of being a
bitch was easy to see through, as much as she wanted to
believe otherwise. Although I hated the thought that I'd
only managed to make progress because she was drunk,
I still chose to view this as a win.

"I'm sorry," she said turning to me, "I know I'm
a bitch. I'd say I can't help it, but I can. I'd say I'll try
harder not to be one, but I won't. However, just because
I've accepted I'm a horrible person doesn't mean I rel-
ish in hurting people and am too proud to apologize. So

again, I'm sorry. Hopefully when we wake up tomorrow we can just put all this behind us."

"I accept your apology. But you're wrong."

"I know. I have no idea the IQ level of the women you date and I shouldn't have assumed as much. Based on what I know of you so far, it's easy to see that you could obviously find a woman who is the whole package."

"Thank you, but that's not what you're wrong about." Ah, that got her attention. Her eyebrow rose and she looked at me with confused annoyance. I didn't give her a chance for a smart ass reply this time. "You aren't a horrible person. And you're not a bitch. There is a reason you put on this don't-give-a-shit front, and I'm going to find out why. Eventually you'll see that you can be real with me, Adalyn. You can keep trying to push me away, but I happen to enjoy a good challenge."

"Oh, so that's your game," she snapped at me, and without having to look I could feel her piercing eyes. "I don't cream my pants at the sight of you and you can't stand that. Are you seriously so cocky that it's so unfathomable that a woman wouldn't be interested in you? You want to know why I'm a bitch? It's for that exact reason. Assholes like you who think your games don't have the power to destroy people."

"Another piece of the puzzle. I take that to mean that some dumbass has done that to you in the past? You can elaborate on that later, but let me assure you, that's not what's happening here. Is it so hard to believe that I find you interesting and want to get to know you?"

"Yes."

"Why?"

Silence. I could tell she wasn't going to say any thing more, so I dropped the subject. For now. I'd already gained valuable insight from this little exchange alone. Apparently the trick was to keep her talking, if you could keep her in one place for long enough, that is. She had made a bad habit of running away from me already. For someone who was so obviously guarded, she wasn't very good at hiding her feelings. It may not be intentional, but my guess would be that deep down she's desperate for someone to really understand her.

With that thought, I realized it was time to admit to myself that I was already in way too deep when it came to Adalyn, and I had no plans of getting out.

It wasn't until I pulled up to her apartment that it dawned on me. Her purse was stolen. That meant we didn't have a key to get in. She was already starting to unbuckle her seat belt.

"Slow down there, Sunshine. You're coming home with me. We…"

"The HELL I am," she interrupted before I could

explain. "I don't know who the hell you think you are, but I am not near drunk enough to sleep with you. I was actually starting to think you might not be as big of an asshole as I thought you were, but if you're willing to take advantage of someone not in full control of their decisions then you are an even bigger asshole than I originally thought."

"Whoa, calm down. If you had let me finish, I would have explained that you don't have a key. Your purse was stolen, remember? So unless you want to park your cute little ass on the lawn and wait for Stacy to come home God knows when, then you don't have a choice."

You could see her mind working, trying to figure out a way to avoid coming to my place but not have to sleep outside like a homeless person. I think she was actually contemplating sleeping outside, but it was freezing out, so I waited patiently for her to finally give up. After what felt like an hour, she finally huffed a sigh of resignation and sank back into her seat.

"Fine. But if you put your fucking hands on me I will seriously have your ass thrown in jail. You get to sleep on the couch while I sleep in your room with the door locked. I don't want you trying to sneak a peek at my lady bits while I'm sleeping."

"Lady bits?" She actually smiled a little. It was brief and was barely noticeable, but I still saw it. "Don't worry, Sunshine. I'd love to have you in my bed, any way I can get you."

Chuckling when she groaned in response, I turned the corner and headed to my apartment.

Adalyn was passed out before I made it halfway to my apartment. I didn't have the heart to wake her, so when we pulled up to the front I handed the valet my keys and turned to scoop her up. The bellman gave me a questioning look, no doubt thinking my carrying in a woman clearly passed out into the building was bizarre. I'd never had a woman here, let alone an unconscious one.

Getting my apartment door unlocked without dropping her was somewhat of a challenge, but once I managed to make it inside, I carried her straight to my room. Yeah, I had two really nice guest rooms that had never been used that I could put her in, but I liked the idea of her in my bed. As much as I wished I was going to be in that bed with her, just having her in there, knowing the next time I laid down her scent would still linger was enough to make my cock hard.

Down boy. Now's not the time.

She mumbled something I couldn't understand as I laid her down, but I could hear it clearly the second time as she rolled over. My name. And if hearing my name come off her lips while she lay in my bed wasn't enough to make my soldier stand at attention, then the moan that followed it definitely was. Was she having a naughty dream about me?

It took every ounce of self-restraint I had, but I managed to pull the covers over her and retreat from my bedroom with one last glance. I may have been trying to prove how much of a gentleman I could be, but I was still a man and leaving her in there after hearing the sounds I'd just heard was extremely difficult, to say the least.

Pulling a couple of blankets and a pillow from the linen closet, I started to make my bed on the couch. Sure, I could have used one of the guest rooms, but Adalyn had demanded I sleep on the couch and I didn't want her to wake and not know where I was. I knew she would feel better knowing where to find me and knowing I had listened and obeyed her demands.

I had no idea what would happen in the morning. Multiple scenarios ran through my head as I lay there, staring at the ceiling. She could wake up embarrassed by the events that happened tonight, though I doubt that would happen. Even if she was embarrassed she wouldn't let me know it. She was hands down the most stubborn woman I had ever met.

She could wake up with no memory what-so-ever, but I didn't think she was drunk enough to completely black out everything. No, my bet was on her waking up angry. Chances were, as soon as she woke up and realized she was in my bed and started to remember everything, she would come storming out there demanding I take her home. Or maybe she would just storm out without a word.

I'd never met someone so unpredictable. Under any other circumstances, being subjected to these types of unforeseen mood swings would test my patience to no end. But Adalyn wasn't like any other woman I'd ever met. As I drifted off to sleep with a smile on my face, anxious to see what tomorrow would bring, I couldn't help but think that it had only taken this girl less than twelve hours to flip my life completely upside down.

CHAPTER 10

ADALYN

Shit.

Dammit.

I was such an idiot.

I sat in Ian's bed for well over a half an hour, internally cursing at myself for drinking the night before. I remembered most of it, but there were enough fuzzy parts for me to know that I could have been missing vital pieces of information. I went back and forth over whether or not I even wanted to fill in the gaps.

After internally berating myself, I turned my thoughts to Ian. He really was remarkable last night. No matter how many times I tried to keep reminding myself that he was no different than all the other assholes I'd met, he kept finding ways to prove me wrong. Fighting the urge to open up to this man was becoming a constant battle of wills. I'd known him less than 24 hours, and in that little amount of time I had managed to be the biggest bitch to him. Even bitchier than I even thought I was capable of. With anyone else, I would actually be proud of myself for that, but after last night all I felt was guilt.

The guilt didn't last long though, quickly being replaced with confusion. Why was he doing this? Why weren't my normal tactics pushing him away? He was dangerously perceptive and was figuring me out much more quickly than I was comfortable with. I wanted to choose when people got to know me, I didn't want to be tricked or manipulated into a relationship. Not that he would want any kind of relationship with me. But if he wasn't interested in me, why would he keep pushing me?

Games. It's always a game.

Either way, he was a close friend of Stacy's and whether or not his motives were genuine, he still took care of me last night and like it or not, I owed him for that. Hopefully he didn't expect more than a simple 'thank you' as a means of showing my gratitude, otherwise he would be in for a huge let down.

Deciding it was time to face the music, I got up to find Ian. And hopefully some aspirin and a gallon of water. First things first, though. Bathroom. After relieving myself I chanced a look in the mirror and almost screamed in horror. I didn't just have panda eyes, I had black makeup running literally all down my face. My hair looked like the only thing that could salvage it was a weed whacker. I wasn't super self conscious about my appearance, but this was just unacceptable.

Considering that Ian had been trying to force me to be 'comfortable' around him, I decided to do just that. Get comfortable. I helped myself to a shower, used his toothbrush and hairbrush and stole some clothes. I even used his deodorant. I smelled exactly like him. Between the shampoo, deodorant and his clothes, I was literally engulfed with Ian's scent.

Yep. I was just going to ignore those butterflies that I got from that thought.

After taking my time getting cleaned up I finally navigated my way to living room, but I immediately stopped, frozen in place. I couldn't believe what was in front of my eyes. Was I in Ian's apartment? I mean, I remembered him saying that's where he was taking me, and I could see him laying on the couch, but this surely couldn't be where he lived. I saw his office, and this had to be the exact opposite.

It was a large, open room with high ceilings, and I could see the kitchen and dining area off to the left. The massive size was not what shocked me though, it's what was all over the walls and filling the room that caused my jaw to drop. Every wall was covered in a bright paint, none of them matching the other. The largest wall in the living room had a mural covering it in what looked to be street art. Photographs, framed posters and canvases covered large portions of the other walls. It was a hodge podge of art to the extreme, nothing matching anything else in the room.

Then spread out sporadically throughout the space were vintage video games. The ones you find in arcades, but they were all the classics. The dining room table was clearly not being used for entertainment, at least not the traditional kind. It was covered in Legos. LEGOS! To the right of it was the biggest television I had ever seen, underneath of which appeared to be some sort of shrine to video games.

It was by far the most bizarre bachelor pad I'd ever seen. I knew "boys and their toys" was a thing but this was to the extreme. Did I just step into a scene from the movie 'Big'? If I found a giant floor piano and a trampoline in this place, then I would be convinced I'd died and was spending the rest of eternity with Tom Hanks reliving a childhood fantasy.

Then it hit me. Did he have a kid? That would complicate things exponentially. Wait. No it wouldn't. Only if I were thinking about dating Ian would it complicate things. And I was definitely NOT thinking about dating Ian...at all.

I didn't even realize I had made my way over to him, but before I could stop myself I was shaking Ian awake. I still hadn't managed to close my jaw and form any type of expression other than shock and awe, but Lord help me, I was just stuck in a state of surprise.

"Where are we, Ian?"

"We're at my apartment. I told you I was bringing you here, remember?" He groaned, his voice muffled from being pressed against a pillow.

"This is YOUR apartment? Are you shitting me right now?"

"I know what you're thinking, and it's why I never bring women here. It looks juvenile and I've never felt like having to explain myself, so if you could keep this between us I would appreciate it."

I finally looked down at him as he was sitting up, rubbing his face with the palm of his hands. He was wearing loose sweat pants and no shirt or socks. Holy Hell in a hamster wheel, if my jaw dropped any further then it might dislocate itself. You could easily tell by looking at him in clothes that he was fit, but nothing prepared me for seeing him without a shirt. I didn't think I'd seen that type of perfection unless it was photoshopped.

Sitting there, half naked on his couch, he wasn't as intimidating somehow. I didn't realize until just then exactly how he really affected me. Especially when he was in his power suit, perfectly tailored to fit his toned body. He was the epitome of success and power. Everything I loathed in a man. Yet here, he just seemed…. normal.

Suddenly, I found it damn near impossible to resist reaching out and touching him. I wanted to run my fingers through his gorgeous hair, feel it's silkiness between my fingers. I was still in so much shock from his apartment and his glorious abs that I had even less control over myself than I did when I was drunk.

Before I could stop myself, I pushed my fingers through his hair. It felt even better than I imagined and a moan slipped out of my mouth involuntarily. He jerked his head up from my unexpected touch and I could see clearly on his face what he was feeling. Desire. Not just desire, but pure, unadulterated lust. His tight jaw told me he was forcing himself to stay still, the muscles on his forearms twitched from fighting the urge to reach out and touch me.

I should be questioning that line of thinking. I should have been warning myself to be careful, reminding myself that it wasn't possible for him to have those feelings towards me. That feeling anything towards him wasn't safe. But before I could force myself back to reality, I felt his big hands pulling me down, straddling me over his lap. My hand was still in his hair, the other placed firmly on his shoulder. One of his hands was placed firmly on my hip while his other hand found it's way around the back of my neck.

I wanted to resist. I should have resisted. I knew what would happen if I didn't stop both us. *Pain.* Not right then, right then would be glorious. But later, when he grew bored with me or realized that I couldn't satisfy him like he wanted, that's when the pain would come. As the harsh truth of those thoughts started to send signals to the rest of my body, warning me to stop, he broke my train of thought by crashing his lips to mine.

I froze at first, tightening every muscle in my body, but his mouth was gentle and warm. Involuntarily, my body relaxed and my lips had a mind of their own. His tongue started gently massaging my lower lip, coaxing, begging for an invitation. The throbbing between my legs won the battle over my logic, and with the proverbial snap of a finger, all inhibitions were lost.

CHAPTER 11

IAN

Her mouth on mine felt even better than I imagined it would. The kiss started off gentle, but quickly became hungry and rough, as if she were afraid slowing down would give her too much time to overthink what was happening. I pulled away and stared into her eyes, desperate to see the same need I was feeling reflected in them. Her chest was heaving up and down with harsh breaths and a myriad of emotions played across her face. Hunger. Fear. Pain? Before I could ask, my phone rang. I was going to ignore it, but I could tell by the expression on her face that the moment was broken. She was already shutting down, putting the walls back up and closing herself off to me.

Dammit!

"What!?" I yelled into phone.

"Well fuck you very much, asshole."

"Stacy?"

"Yeah it's me, dumbass."

"Is that Stacy? Is she okay?" Adalyn asked me while straightening her clothes, inching further away from me. *Wait, those weren't her clothes.* Were those MY clothes? She offered me an apologetic smile when she saw me eyeing the baggy pants and t-shirt that hung loosely from her body. I didn't even bother trying to hide the smile it gave me, thinking of her making herself comfortable in my home. I had been so wrapped up in the feel of her when she put her fingers through my hair that I didn't even notice that her own hair was wet. Visions of Adalyn, wet in my shower, flashed through my mind and I turned slightly in an attempt to conceal how much our kiss and the fantasy of a wet, naked Adalyn were turning me on.

"Is that Adalyn? Where are you? Why are you together? You know what, bigger shit to deal with right now. Put her on the phone."

"Stacy, where are…"

"Put her on the fucking phone, Ian!"

Handing my phone to Adalyn, I headed to the kitchen for a drink of water, trying like hell to fight the disappointment taking over me, wishing I could just go back 20 minutes and put my damn phone on silent.

CHAPTER 12

ADALYN

"Okay listen, I don't have much time, but I'm telling you now that you and I are going to discuss this shit later and don't even think of getting out of it. You are going to tell me every detail of the last twelve hours you spent with Ian. But right now, I need you to come get me out of jail."

"WHAT!? Why are you still in jail? I thought that cop was just messing with you."

"Ha! Yeah, apparently the dickwad failed to mention that his shift was ending. He brought me here and fucking left. HE LEFT! And the rest of these assholes said they couldn't release me because Officer Fuckwad brought me in and hadn't done any paperwork and so I had to wait for him to get back. Though they were laughing the whole time so who knows if that's even true."

I could hear a muffled man's voice in the background.

"Yeah, FUCK YOU pencil dick. What are you gonna do? Arrest me for calling you on your bullshit? Last I checked, you can't keep me here just because you don't like me. This is a clear abuse of your power. I hope you know I'm going to make your life fucking miserable for this."

Oh my god. Was she seriously threatening a cop? While she was in JAIL?! Oh shit. Oh shit. What if she gets tasered. The image of Stacy writhing around on the ground because one of the officer's got sick of her attitude was actually pretty hysterical. Somehow I managed to keep myself from laughing.

"Stacy, please tell me you aren't talking to a police officer."

"No, I'm not talking to a police officer. I'm talking to THREE of them. And they are all fucking pricks." She sounded angry but I could have sworn I heard her laugh after another muffled male voice chimed in. "Unless one or all of you sexy bastards want to come over here and strip search me and fulfill a lifelong fantasy of mine, then you should probably shut the hell up." She mumbled something else into the phone, but it was muffled I couldn't understand it.

"Listen, Stacy. We're on our way. Just please, please try not to do anything stupid. Please."

"Yeah, yeah whatever. Just get your cute ass down here and get me out of this place before I start tearing off all my clothes and dry humping the bars to my cell. These cops may be jerks but they are seriously hot, and you know how I get around hot jerks."

It didn't take long to find Stacy. We followed the sound

of her voice. By the time we reached her, she had been let out of the cell and was standing off to the side talking to a couple of officers. She had dialed down the bitchiness and turned up the charm, and these unsuspecting souls were already under her spell. I cleared my throat and she turned to face me, then ran over and hugged me. Then she punched me.

"What the hell was that for?" I asked, rubbing my arm. She'd hit me hard enough that I knew it would bruise.

"For letting that prick of a cop bring me here last night."

"Um, Stacy. He's a police officer. What did you expect me to do? If I would have tried to stop him then I would have ended up in here with you."

"Yeah, but at least I wouldn't have been alone. That was the longest night of my life. And what if he *had* let me go later in the night? You would have just left me stranded with no way to get home? What if something bad happened to me?!"

"First of all, don't even try to pretend like you didn't enjoy yourself. Second of all, I highly doubt an entire precinct of policeman would have let something bad happen to you. Surely you've managed to make a friend while you were in here." Instead of responding to me, Stacy turned and winked at one of the officers she had just been talking to.

Just then the officer from last night walked in, wearing a shit eating grin. I could feel Stacy's anger vibrating off of her as she stood next to me, and she growled. Loudly. Not one of those low, barely audible growls. No, she was growling at him like a warning, telling him if he came too close she would whip out her claws and scratch his eyes out.

The officer Stacy had just winked at walked over to us and introduced himself as Joe, who was apparently the arresting officer's partner.

"Don't listen to Stacy, I kept her company all night. She had a great time," he said as he winked back at Stacy. "Chad's not a bad guy, he just has a low tolerance for drunk chicks and their shenanigans." Stacy punched his arm and they started to bicker playfully. They were acting as if they'd known each other for years. Not that unusual for Stacy to make friends, but it was unusual that their banter sounded completely friendly and platonic. Joe was extremely attractive and Stacy not flirting with him was strange.

Putting that curiosity aside to ask Stacy about later, I walked up to the desk to file my report. It was going to be such a pain getting all my credit cards cancelled and reissued and I'd have to get a new phone. Dammit. I really needed to get a job. It was time to quit stalling and start trying to figure out what to do with my life.

CHAPTER 13

IAN

While the girls dealt with the police, I made some calls off to the side. Eventually I had to step out so I could hear over Stacy's yelling. She's naturally pretty confrontational but I'd never seen anyone get under her skin the way this officer did. About a half hour later, I had to literally drag Stacy out of the station with us while she flailed her arms around, shooting empty threats of violence against a station full of law enforcement. Crazy dumbass.

Stacy was practically a sister to me and we'd been friends as long as I could remember. Carrie and I practically lived at her house when we were young. Our parents used to fight constantly, then after our dad left us, our mom became really depressed. She wouldn't get out of bed for days and we would never have food to eat in our house, so Stacy's mom had kind of taken us in as her own and when we weren't at school we were at her house, only going home to sleep.

About a year after our dad left, mom got really sick. Her symptoms weren't as obvious at first because she had started drinking, but when it started to become obvious something was really wrong I begged her to see a doctor, but she wouldn't go. It wasn't until she actually passed away three years after my dad had left that we found out what was even wrong with her.

I managed to make it through high school while trying to take care of my mom and Carrie, but my grades had suffered because of it. Because I was only fifteen when our dad left I had been forced to grow up very quickly. He sent money every month, so I took over managing the bills, so at least we weren't completely homeless since most days our mom wouldn't even get out of bed.

Our mom died when I was eighteen, so I petitioned the court for guardianship of Carrie. We continued to live off of our dad's monthly payments, but we didn't need much and I put most of it aside in an account for Carrie to use for college or whatever she would need later. We continued to spend most of our time at Stacy's house and we were thankful for the home cooked meals.

If it weren't for Stacy and her mom, that time of our lives definitely would have been a lot more difficult. I did as much as I could to be a father figure to Carrie, but I was still very much a kid myself. I worried constantly about her, trying to watch for signs of depression, not wanting her to end up like our mom. One of her passions was dancing and I made sure she was still able to continue pursuing that even when everything was falling apart. Carrie managed to make it through high school with good grades and ended up going to school for dance. I couldn't have been more proud of her than I was.

And none of that could have happened without Stacy. Stacy was our rock, standing by our side through everything. Even with how young her and Carrie were when our dad left, Stacy always seemed to know the right things to say and could tell when we just wanted to pretend everything was normal. She was our only family, so even as I sat in the car listening to her rant about her night in jail, I knew I'd do anything for her. Which might soon include bailing her out of jail for assaulting a police officer.

Snapping out of my reverie, I tuned in to hear the girls complaining about how hungry they were. I turned to ask Adalyn where she wanted to eat and Stacy pushed her way up from my backseat and stuck her head in between us. "I don't care where we go, but I want some fucking pancakes. And I want them stat, so stop eye fucking each other and get going."

Adalyn just rolled her eyes and I laughed under my breath while Stacy threw herself back, crossing her arms over her chest. All I could think about was that moment in my apartment right before Stacy called. The way Adalyn was looking at me and how amazing her lips felt against mine. I'd had my fair share of women and some of them had been extremely gorgeous and really great in bed, but I had never wanted any of them as much as I wanted Adalyn. I'd never really wanted any of them for more than a night. They were a means to end, a scratch to an itch. I wanted so much more from Adalyn than just one night, even though I knew it would be amazing.

I shifted in my seat, trying to discretely rearrange my cock, now hard from the thought of Adalyn naked in my bed. I wasn't discreet enough, though, because I could see Adalyn's mouth twitch into a smile before she quickly looked away. I wanted to reach over and twine my fingers through hers, desperate for some sort of physical contact, but remembering Stacy was with us I decided against it. Whatever was happening with Adalyn was fragile, and I didn't want to put pressure on her. For all I knew she regretted kissing me, though the smile still lingering on her lips as she quietly stared out the window told me otherwise.

The next hour was the most enjoyable I'd had in a while. Just sitting back, listening as Stacy recounted the previous night's events to Adalyn, getting to watch Adalyn's face light up and the laughter flow so easily was causing my chest to tighten. She looked so happy and carefree. I wanted to be the one making her look that way.

I knew I should be terrified by the intense feelings I was already having for Adalyn, but I couldn't bring myself to let my mind go there. Having spent so much of my life focused on my career, I found I was ready to put my focus somewhere else for once. But not just some-

where, on some*one*. I could reason away my attraction to her, find excuses as to why I was already growing so attached, but my instincts had gotten me this far in life. Anything worth having involved risks. Everything I had, I had earned by pushing limits, being determined and by taking risks on things other people found to be insane or unreasonable.

So even though this girl already had the ability to completely crush me, I knew it was worth it. I didn't do regrets, and not pursuing Adalyn would undoubtedly be a regret I would have to live with for the rest of my life.

I realized I had just been sitting there like a dumbass, not saying anything the entire time, when I could have been using this opportunity to get to know Adalyn. So as soon as there was a lull in the conversation, I made my move.

"So Adalyn, Stacy has shown me some of your artwork. It's pretty phenomenal. Did you go to college for art?"

Adalyn, who was sitting directly across from me, choked on her water and Stacy, who was sitting next to her, started pounding on her back. It took several seconds for Adalyn to get her coughing settled down and she finally looked up at me, looking slightly embarrassed.

"Sorry, wrong pipe," she finally said as she cleared her throat. "No, I didn't study art in college. I mean, I took some classes and originally I had planned to major in music education with a minor in art history, but after the ra…the uh…once it came time to make a decision I figured it would be smarter of me to pick something that would give me more options when it came time to start a career." She let out a self deprecating laugh and shook her head. "It backfired in the end. I still haven't been able to find anything I'm passionate about enough to make a career out of."

"Well, I'm no art buff by any means, but from what I saw, you have some serious talent. I'm sure there is a way for you to put that talent to use in the work force. Have you thought about looking for jobs at museums or art galleries?"

"Yeah, I thought about it, but I'm more of a do-er, so just standing around selling someone else's stuff really sounds more like torture than anything. And honestly, I kind of left that part of me behind. It's more of a hobby than anything."

"Well, that's a shame. Keeping all your beauty from the world like that seems like an injustice." She tilted her head to the side and smiled coyly at me. "I mean the beauty of your paintings, not you yourself. Not that you aren't beautiful, because you are. You're extremely beautiful. Breathtakingly beautiful. I just meant that… dammit, I'm just going to shut up now."

Adalyn giggled at my rambling and gave me a shy smile. The spark in her eyes and the change in her demeanor just in the last day had changed so drastically, and this shy side of Adalyn was adorable. Yeah, I still had some walls to break through, but I was a patient man. It was time to put into action my plan to win over the girl in front of me who unknowingly already possessed my heart.

Chapter 14

Adalyn

After spending two excruciating hours at my bank, canceling my cards and switching over my account numbers to be safe, I finally had all of that sorted out. Problem was, my checking account was dwindling fast and I didn't have credit cards to rely on until they came in the mail.

I'd spent all day Sunday nursing a hangover with Stacy. Ian had dropped us off after breakfast and for a second I thought he might lean over and kiss me, but Stacy and her oblivious ass shoved her face in between us spouting off about the cop that arrested her. She hadn't stopped talking about him since we picked her up. I thought she would calm down with time but the more she ranted over it, the worse she got.

So first thing Monday morning, I set out to replace everything that had been stolen. My purse hadn't shown up at the club, so I had no choice but to just cancel everything and replace it all. Only I didn't have enough to buy a new phone and my insurance had ran out. What did that mean? It meant I was done screwing around and needed to find a job. ASAP.

Knowing this was coming, I'd spent part of Sunday afternoon, the day before, going through the want ads and circling potential jobs. After spending the remainder of the day sending out resumes and making calls, I had lined up three job interviews for the next day. I just prayed one of them would hire me, and soon, because this being poor shit was getting old.

By the time I made it back to Stacy's apartment late on Tuesday, I was beat and in desperate need of chocolate. A glass of wine would probably work better, but I had learned my lesson at Grind. When Stacy got home from work about a half an hour after me, she threw her bags on the floor, her stuff scattering everywhere. She was such a slob. I loved her anyway.

"What are you doing lying on the couch in sweatpants eating a candy bar? You're way too young to give up, Addy. Seriously, you're a hot mess."

"Well, hello to you too, bitch."

"How did your job interviews go?"

"How do you think they went? Do you think I normally celebrate in ratty pajamas, stuffing my face with empty calories while I watch reruns of Married With Children?"

"I'm sorry, Addy. You'll find something," Stacy tried to console me, plopping down on the couch next to me, almost knocking me over.

"Why do you love getting in my personal space?

You are a special kind of evil, you know that, right?"

Stacy just grinned wickedly and snatched the candy bar out of my hands. "Hey! Give that back!" We wrestled for a minute on the couch, fighting over the candy bar, before I finally gave up and scooted further down the couch, crossing my arms and pouting.

"Don't take your shit out on me, Addy. You know the answer to your problems, you're just too stubborn to accept it."

"I'm not going to interview with Ian."

"I don't understand why not. He'll give you the job, the interview's just a formality. I'm sure it pays well and you're kind of desperate, probably in more ways than one," she joked, nudging me with her elbow. "I bet he could help you with both."

I smacked her in the face with a throw pillow. "I hate you."

"You love me. Now take my phone and call Ian and set up that interview."

Ugh. She was right, I had no other options. Not if I wanted a job any time soon. I pinched her and then jumped off the couch when she tried to pinch me back, barely making my escape. She threw the candy bar at me right as the phone starting ringing. I was still laughing when Ian answered.

"Stace? What's up?"

"Oh, um, actually, it's Adalyn."

There was a long pause. I checked to see if the phone had been disconnected, but it still showed the call on her screen. "Hello?"

"Sorry, I just wasn't expecting it to be you Adalyn. I was surprised. Is everything okay? Why are you calling from Stacy's phone?"

"Oh, I um, I haven't had mine replaced yet so Stacy let me borrow hers to call you and see if, um, if maybe…" Why couldn't I get the words out? It was so much easier to be confident when I was face to face with him. It didn't make any sense because he was so handsome it almost hurt to look at him, but being able to see him reminded me of the type of guy he was. The kind I avoided.

"I just…I was wondering if that position was still open at your company? I was hoping maybe…maybe you would still let me interview? If I haven't already ruined that opportunity after the first time we met."

Another pause. Was I interrupting something? He seemed distracted. Or at least from what I could tell over the phone, anyway.

"Ian?"

"No," he said, clearing his throat. "I mean, you didn't ruin anything. Of course I would be happy to bring you in for an interview. Can you meet tomorrow morning? I had a meeting cancel at 9 a.m. so that would be a good time for me. There is a coffee shop across the street from my office, so we could meet there."

"Oh, yes, of course. Thank you. I'll be there at 9. Thank you."

Another long pause. This was the most awkward phone conversation I think I'd ever had.

"Adalyn?"

"Yes?"

"I look forward to tomorrow."

And then he was gone.

"Adalyn, you look great. Stop stressing over this. I told you, Ian's going to give you the job no matter what."

Stacy was sitting on my bed, lecturing me. Why was lecturing me one of her favorite pastimes? She was seriously annoying sometimes. I threw my hair brush at her but she dodged it at the last second.

"Don't throw shit at me! I'm trying to help you!"

Looking in the mirror, pushing one last stray hair back into place, I sighed and exited the bathroom. "I know Stacy, but I don't want a job that I didn't earn. I don't even know what his company does. What does he do anyway?"

Waving her hand at me dismissively, she downed the rest of her disgusting kale wheatgrass something-or-other nasty smoothie. "I don't know, I never understand when he explains. Something to do with making stuff."

"Well that's vague. If you don't even know what

he does then how do you know I'd be a good fit there?"

I started to make my way to the living room to drink a quick cup of coffee before heading out to meet with Ian and Stacy followed.

"I know it requires being creative and I don't know anyone more creative than you."

"You just don't know very many people, Stacy," I laughed, shaking my head at her. Stacy had always been my biggest cheerleader.

"Whatever, you know that's not what I meant. Look, you may not want the job, but you have to at least meet with him. You never know."

Slipping on my heels, I let out a heavy sigh. "I know, Stace, I know. Thank you for getting me this interview. I'll text you later and let you know how it goes." She started towards me with her arms open, so I turned and bolted out the door.

"Nice try, Stacy!" I yelled as I ran down the hallway. I hated hugs.

"Good luck, whore!"

It was a nice day out so I decided to walk. The coffee shop we were meeting at was only four blocks away and I had left plenty early. I thought the fresh air would help me clear my head and prepare for whatever was about to happen.

Things with Ian were tense, at best. I hadn't heard from him since the day he dropped me off after staying over at his place. I wanted to tell myself that if I had a phone, he would have been trying to call or text me, but who knows if that's true. I'm not even sure if I would want that.

There was something different about Ian. I got the feeling that my initial judgment of him may have been a little off. Of course I saw the expensive suit and his perfectly defined body and panty dropping smile, so I assumed what any woman would. That he was a chauvinistic, cocky bastard. Okay, maybe not all women would jump to that exact conclusion, but I had.

Not that my instincts were to be trusted nowadays. But even if Ian was a great guy and I had been wrong, I wasn't in any kind of place to be dating someone. I was still trying to work out my own crap, not to mention finding a job and figuring out the basics.

Of course I was sexually attracted to Ian. There isn't a woman alive who could resist that man. With his perfectly chiseled face, dark hair, dark eyes and million-watt-smile. Just thinking about him made me shiver. But he was close with Stacy, so no matter how much I wanted him, I couldn't sleep with him. It wouldn't end well for anyone.

When I approached the cafe I spotted Ian already inside, sitting at a table in the far corner. As I walked in the door chimed and he looked up and smiled. That smile. Pretending to not be affected by that smile was getting harder and harder. Resisting the urge to reach up and fan myself from the sudden wave of heat I felt rush through my body, I forced a polite smile and made my way towards him.

He stood up as I neared the table and pulled out my chair. Such a gentleman. "Good morning, Adalyn. Thank you for meeting me here. Sometimes I like to do interviews outside of the office. It's more casual and it's easier to have honest conversations when you're relaxed. Can I get you something to drink?"

"Oh, um, no thank you. I had coffee before I left." He tilted his head to the side and looked at me quizzically. Probably wondering why I drank coffee when I knew I was going to a coffee house. Truth was I was too afraid I'd spill it all over myself or do something embarrassing. Interviews were hard enough, but sitting here with Ian was almost unbearable.

Pulling my resume out of my bag, I handed it to him and started to give him a little back ground of my education and job experience. "As you can see, I have experience in many areas. Everything from clerical work to manual labor. I'll try just about anything once. I have…"

He held up a hand cutting me off mid sentence. "Why have you had so many jobs in such a short amount of time? There has to be at least 15 employers here from the last two years alone. I expect loyalty and long term commitment from my employees, is that going to be a problem?"

This was the worst part. This was the part where I lost any chance I had at landing a job. There were no good answers for this. No matter what story I gave I still ended up looking bad. I started to tell him the fake story, but I quickly shut my mouth when I saw his expression. He wasn't looking at me with judgment, just curiosity. Something about him in that moment made me want to tell him the truth. And before I could stop myself, I did.

"I don't really know what I want to do with my life. I've been trying different things, hoping to find something I'm passionate about, but I haven't found it yet. Most of the time I either get bored and leave or I have... conflicts...with my superiors that results in my termination. I can assure you though, I work hard and I will do a good job, no matter the task."

"Until you get bored, right?" My shoulders tensed and my defensive instincts kicked in, but when he winked at me, I instantly relaxed again. "Tell me what you mean by conflicts with your superiors."

"I have...difficulty...with control. I don't like to be held to a certain standard, given specific expectations, or to be put in a box with people they assume are just like me. I like to be independent, creative, push boundaries. I'm not content to just follow orders and do as I'm told."

His lip curled up on one side and I could tell he was fighting a smile. "I know, it's unrealistic. Everyone has to answer to someone in some shape, way or form. It's an issue I'm working on. But I definitely thrive more in a position where I'm given more freedoms."

Ian nodded his head several times, taking in what I'd said. I just waited. Waited for the inevitable where he told me I wouldn't be a good fit. What he did next surprised me.

"Come with me," he said, pulling me up from my seat and leading me towards the door.

"What? Where are we going?"

When we got to his car, he opened the passenger side door and turned to look at me. "I think you would be a great fit for my company, Adalyn. I can tell by the look you're giving me right now that you don't believe me. And I think the only way to prove to you that you would be an asset is to show you exactly what my company does. So get in, we need to run by your apartment."

Stumbling into the seat, I buckled my seatbelt as Ian rounded the car. "Why do we need to go by my apartment?" I asked as he started the car and pulled away.

"You need a change of clothes. You're going to want something more comfortable." The confusion on my face had to be obvious. He was making absolutely no sense. "Trust me," he said smiling at me. "You'll see."

CHAPTER 15

IAN

I waited in the car while Adalyn ran into her apartment to get a change of clothes. The position I was actually looking to fill was secretarial, but now knowing how much Adalyn hates the mundane, I knew she wouldn't be a good fit there.

Stacy had shown me some of Adalyn's art and even let me listen to a few songs she had written. I knew she had talent and would be beneficial to my creative team. We didn't need anyone else in that area right now, but I'd be damned if I was going to let her get away. I could come up with a way to integrate her into the team.

I was handling this all wrong. There were protocols that were to be followed when hiring someone for the creative team, but I knew if I started making Adalyn sign contracts before she even understood what we do then she would bolt. Handing her documents full of rules and stipulations before ever explaining anything did not sound like something that would go over well.

I found myself bouncing my leg up and down anxiously, tapping the steering wheel incessantly. It felt like she had been gone for an hour, but looking at the time on my phone it had only been five minutes. Just as I thought I was going to lose it if I had to sit there any longer, she emerged from the building carrying a small duffle bag.

"Buckle up, Sunshine," I said as she slid back into the passenger seat.

"I don't think calling me annoying nicknames is entirely appropriate during an interview, Ian. Assuming this is still an interview after the bizarre turn of events."

"Ian, I seriously hate this building," Adalyn said to me with a look of disgust as we entered the main lobby.

"So, tell me then, what would you do to make it better?"

"Well, first thing I would do is remove everything in here and then replace it all."

"Oh, well if that's all I need to do then I'll just get right on it."

I liked this playful Adalyn. I felt like she was finally starting to be more comfortable around me. I could tell she was still guarding herself, but I was hoping that once she saw my main work space that maybe that would change. I had no way of knowing how she would react once we got up there, but my instincts told me she would like it. At least I hoped she would.

Stopping her just before the elevators, I gently pulled her to the side, out of the way.

"Before we go up there, let me explain a little bit about what we do here. We are creators. Not to be confused with inventors. We don't invent entirely new products. We take existing products and make them better, expand on them or develop a similar product but with improvements. Companies come to us for re-branding and product makeovers. We specialize in entertainment, mostly in recreational types of products."

"Okay...I don't know if that explanation made it better or worse. I still have no idea what you do here, and what all of that would have to do with me needing a change of clothes."

"You're right, there really is no way of explaining it. Best I can do is show you. So, let's head on up."

We rode up to my main office on the fortieth floor in silence. Despite how large the elevator was, we both stood very close to each other, our shoulders almost touching. I could smell her sweet perfume and could hear her breathing, slightly faster than normal. When our hands brushed against each other her breathing picked up even more and I risked a glance at her. She noticed my movement and glanced up at me returning my smile.

I wanted so badly to twine my fingers through hers, pull her chest flush to my body and press my lips to hers. After our kiss at my apartment I hadn't been able to stop thinking about tasting her again. I knew her working here would complicate things, but I couldn't pass up an opportunity to spend more time with her. I was finally making progress and if what she needed was more time to get to know me and trust me, then I would be patient.

When the elevator came to a stop and the doors opened I heard Adalyn let out a huge sigh. Had she been holding her breath that whole time? Was she as affected by me as I was by her?

I placed my hand on the small of her back and guided her out into the room, and she tensed at the contact but relaxed after a few seconds. When she finally looked up and took in her surroundings I couldn't help but laugh at the astonishment on her face.

"Holy shit, Ian. What is this place?"

"This is the game room."

"You say that like it's supposed to clear things up for me. I thought we were going to your office. This looks like an arcade," she said in awe, spinning in circles and touching everything. She ran her fingers down a vintage pinball machine to the right of the room and then plopped down onto one of the bean bag chairs that were laying around sporadically throughout the room.

"Think of this as one of the employee break rooms."

"Hold up. First of all, this is just one of the break rooms? Second of all, who has an entire game room as a break room?"

Extending my hand to her to help her stand, I took the duffle bag from her and slung it over my shoulder. "Come on, let me show you around. It will start to make more sense."

The room was expansive, and several employees were taking advantage of it's perks. There was a full kitchen to the left that was fully stocked with every kind of beverage and food you could imagine. In each corner of the room were different table top games; a pool table, a ping pong table, air hockey and even ski ball.

An employee walked over to ask me a question and in the ten seconds it took me to answer them, I had already lost Adalyn. I found her playing air hockey with Mitch, one of my developers. She was cracking up and trash talking him, laughing like they were old friends. How had she made a friend already?

I just stood back and watched until the game was over, and after they high fived Adalyn hopped her way back over to me. "Sorry, I heard him say he needed an opponent and I didn't want to leave him hanging."

This woman was an enigma to me. "It's perfectly fine, I want you to be comfortable here. I think you'll find that pretty much everyone here is laid back and easy to get along with. We encourage that type of environment. Stress in our line of work can be detrimental to our progress, so we do everything we can to keep the staff happy while they are here."

I led her down a long corridor, waving and saying pleasantries with my staff as we went.

"I can see why you told me to get a change of clothes. Everyone here is wearing jeans and t-shirts. I look like an idiot in my skirt and heels."

Stopping in front of her, I put her chin between my fingers. "You look beautiful, Adalyn," I said with the most serious and sincere look I could manage. She blushed and looked down, and I cleared my throat remembering I was talking to a potential employee, not a date.

We approached the employee lounge. "This is our lounge area. It has showers, dressing rooms, lockers, free toiletries. Just about anything you need. Go ahead and go change, you'll want more comfortable clothes for this next part. I'll wait out here for you."

A few moments later Adalyn emerged from the lounge wearing tight fitting yoga pants and a fitted pink t-shirt. Her clothes looked like they were painted on her, showing every curve of her perfect body, and I had to fight the stirring feelings that threatened at the sight of her.

I placed my hand on the small of her back again, and guided her to the end of the hall. When we reached the door to our destination I stopped to look at her again.

"One last thing, Adalyn. What you see behind these doors is highly confidential. You are the first employee to have been in this room prior to signing a non-disclosure and a non-compete clause. So I'm trusting that if you don't take the job, you will keep everything you see beyond this door just between us. Do you understand?"

Her eyes widened in surprise, and she swallowed heavily as she nodded in agreement. Taking a deep breath, I opened the door.

Here goes nothin'.

CHAPTER 16

ADALYN

Ian opened a massive red, metal door and I kid you not, it was like walking into Willy Wonka's factory. Only it was toys, not candy. Ian started to talk, but I had already taken off running.

"Oh my gosh, it's one of those giant floor pianos like in the movie 'Big'! I've always wanted to see one of these ever since I saw that movie. It was my favorite when I was a kid. I love Tom Hanks. Can I try it out?" I knew I was rambling and acting foolish, but Ian was laughing and his amused look relaxed me entirely.

"Of course you can try it. It's an exact replica of the one in the movie," he answered, crossing over to push some sort of power button. I didn't waste any time. I was dancing all over that piano like a crazy person.

"So what is this place?" I yelled over the noise I was causing. When I couldn't hear his answer, I stopped bouncing around and walked over to him. He was leaning against the wall with his legs crossed at the ankles and his hands shoved into the pockets of his pants. "Are you going to make me play by myself, or are you going to join me?" I teased.

Ian shook his head and laughed, but started pulling off his jacket. He kicked off his expensive dress shoes, tossed his jacket and tie to the ground and started to un-button his white dress shirt. I felt my breath hitch at the site of him undressing, and all I could think was that I wanted him to keep going. To remove everything. The thought of seeing Ian naked made my stomach flutter and I felt my cheeks flush.

As he undid the last button and shrugged off his dress shirt, I couldn't help the giggle that escaped my lips. "Oh my gosh...what is on your t-shirt? Are you wearing a Superman t-shirt?"

He glanced down, looking almost embarrassed, tugging on the hem of his t-shirt. "Yeah, I mean, you know..." He trailed off, and I playfully punched his arm, not even trying to hide the huge grin on my face.

"Ian Drake, are you a closet nerd?" I teased, laugh-ing when a blush colored his cheeks. "Wow...I can't be-lieve how wrong I was about you."

His face fell and the sadness that overtook it threw me. "I'm sorry, Ian. I owe you an apology. All the things I assumed about you at first are obviously wrong. Way wrong. I shouldn't have made a snap judgment."

"I understand," he cleared his throat, seeming to struggle to make eye contact with me. Was he really that mad at me? I was trying to apologize. "Well, thank you for coming in. I assume you can find your way out," he said as he turned to walk out.

I grabbed his arm, stopping him and his head jerked

around, his eyes staring at my hand on his arm. I quickly pulled away and started fidgeting with my hands. My nervous tick. He was laughing and smiling a minute ago. What caused this sudden shift in his mood?

"Wait…what? Did I do something wrong? I mean… we didn't even discuss the job. I really am sorry I misjudged you, Ian. I…I would like an opportunity to see if I might be a good fit here. If…if you can forgive me." The pleading in my voice was obvious. I needed this job. I wanted this job. I didn't even know what the job was but I knew I wanted it.

"You…you still want to do the interview? You want to work here?" He asked me in disbelief.

"Well, yeah, I mean, this place is awesome. I don't think I'd ever want to leave. Would the job require me to live here? Because I'd be okay with that."

He raised one eyebrow, looking at me quizzically. "Are you being serious right now?"

He was confusing the crap out of me. I obviously was missing something. His behavior was so off. This insecure and timid version of Ian was strange. I found myself wanting to comfort him, to ease whatever it was that was making him feel so unsure. He had no reason to feel anything but confident. He was gorgeous and owned a very successful company that also happened to be the coolest place to work on the planet. What had him so out of sorts?

I placed my hand on his arm again. He looked down, staring at the contact again, but I didn't pull away that time.

"Of course I'm serious, Ian. This place," I gestured around me, "this place is amazing. I still don't even understand what it is you do exactly and I don't know what my job would even be, but I know it has to be great if it's at a place like this. Hell, I'll scrub the toilets if you'll let me come in here and play all day. It's cool if you don't have a place for me to sleep, I'll just build a fort," I winked at him, and his whole body relaxed as he let out a long breath. He'd been holding his breath?

"I can tell something is going on, though, Ian. What am I missing? Why would you not believe I would want to work here?"

He stood there for a long time, looking over my shoulder at nothing. I waited patiently, trying to figure out why pain etched his face all of a sudden. I fought the urge to reach up and rub my fingertips across his furrowed brow and down to his jaw, cupping his face in my hand. He was so beautiful; it was painful not to touch him.

Shaking his head, he snapped out of whatever daze he had drifted into. "I'm sorry, it's not important. I just have a lot on my mind."

"Um, yeah, I'm so not letting you get away with that answer. You've really gone out of your way the last few days to try and force yourself into my life, no matter how much I protested. If I'm going to work here and if we are going to be friends, then I need you to be honest with me."

His expression pulled at my heart strings as he stared into my eyes. He looked so vulnerable. Why was this such a difficult question for him? Since I didn't think pulling him into an embrace would be appropriate, I decided a little sarcasm might do the trick. "What, is this some kind of ruse? Like, you're some creepy child molester and this is how you get kids into your clutches?"

That earned me a smirk. "No, nothing like that." He hesitated again, his smile falling just a little. I was starting to get nervous. Dark clouds took over his thoughts, I could see anger rising. It was almost palpable. I instinctively took a step back, putting distance between us. I wasn't afraid he would hurt me, but I had a feeling whatever was about to happen would require me to keep it together. And when I was so close to Ian, drowning in his scent, warmed by his body, I couldn't think straight.

"Adalyn, I may not be the man you think I am." Okay… he's really not making me feel any better about standing here so close to him. Before I could react, he kept going.

"I don't know how much you know about me. How much you've read in the gossip mags, how much Stacy has told you, whatever rumors you've heard. There are few people in my life who truly know me. Even my closest friends only know as much as I let them. Probably the only people in my life who truly know me are Stacy and my sister. I learned early in my career that being successful came with sacrifices. I have to be very private, which is part of why my employees sign a non-disclosure." He paused, lost in thought again. I wanted to snap my fingers in his face, but I sensed this was a confession of sorts and figured he wouldn't appreciate me giving him attitude right now.

"There is something about you, Adalyn. I can't even explain it. I barely know you, but I want to know you. It's been a long time since I really let someone in, let myself be who I truly am. Being vulnerable is hard for anyone, but it's especially difficult when you've been burned before. I'm not saying I've never faced rejection in my life, but it's been all business for me for a very long time now. The last time I really opened up to someone, it almost broke me." He pulled away and ran his hands through his hair and turned his back to me.

"Why are you telling me all of this, Ian? You barely know me. I've not even really been nice to you. What makes you think I'm worthy of taking a risk on?"

Before I could blink, he turned around to face me again and closed the gap between us. He took my hands in his, our noses almost touching. He was staring right into my eyes, like he was searching. Pleading. Like he could see my soul and was begging me to see his. It was intense and terrifying and… beautiful. Something shifted in me and I wasn't afraid anymore. I wanted to know this man and whatever secrets he held. I wanted to be the one he could trust not to hurt him, even if I couldn't trust him. At least, I couldn't trust him yet.

"I'm telling you this because I know you better than you think, Adalyn. You are fierce and confident and go after what you want, but I see what's behind what you choose to show the world. You're unsure, just like me. You're showing people what you want them to see, not who you really are. There are secrets you keep hidden, too, guarding yourself from pain. But I know how exhausting that is, because I do it too, and I'm tired of keeping it all in. I may not know very much about you, but I already know what matters. I always trust my instincts, and my instincts tell me you are worth the risk."

For once, I had nothing to say. I could feel hot tears pricking the back of my eyes, but I had no idea why. It'd been a long time since I'd cried, since I had let someone see me that vulnerable. But I was defenseless against this kind of honesty. No one had ever seen through me so easily, even Stacy, who knew everything. I had a good poker face, yet somehow this beautiful man had seen right past all my bullshit and could see how broken I was and he still wanted to know me.

The logical part of my brain tried to remind me that

I was at a job interview, not on a date. And I had a feeling whatever he was about to tell me was definitely more personal than any boss should be with his employee. But the pain in his eyes was killing me. Even if it made working here impossible, I couldn't help myself from reaching out to him. I wanted to take away his sadness.

Despite all the defenses I'd perfected over the years to prevent letting someone in like I was about to, I just couldn't bring myself to pull away from him now. Not when I could see how desperately he needed a friend. Needed me.

CHAPTER 17

IAN

Stacy and Carrie told me all the time that I was being overly paranoid and self conscious, always criticizing me for hiding so much of myself. But they didn't know, they weren't there the day everything went down with Maggie. I'd never told anyone what she had said to me, the ways she had truly broken me. Always too ashamed to admit the truth, I just avoided giving any details about the day that almost destroyed my entire future.

I thought finally telling someone the whole truth would be terrifying and difficult, but the warmth in her eyes and feeling her soft hand against my cheek made all my worries and fears dissipate. I'd never wanted or needed someone to understand so badly.

"I started off as a programmer, made an app that ended up taking off. I hadn't really done it thinking it would go anywhere, but people liked it, and before I knew it the money was rolling in. I didn't really know what to do with it, I was only twenty at the time and Carrie was still in high school. I was her legal guardian and our lives up to that point had been...different. I didn't really have anyone to advise me on what to do with my money, so I invested it in a business. Hired a few of my buddies, had a small space at first. Basically we would sit around all day playing. Video games, internet games, board games. There wasn't any kind of recreational activity that we didn't take part in. It was like a dream, getting to play for a living."

I cautiously reached out to her, slipping my hand around hers, waiting for her to pull away, but she didn't. Instead she gripped me tightly and intertwined her fingers through mine. I led her over to a bench that was sitting up against the wall to the far left. When we sat down I started to pull my hand away, but she gripped it tighter, and in that moment I'd never felt more comfortable in my entire life. My pull to Adalyn was stronger than my instinct to protect myself, and so I took the plunge, and finally told the story in it's entirety.

"We wanted to make more, more than just apps. We had a couple little ones that were somewhat successful following my first one, but we had started to get bored with just working on those. It surprised me how much I enjoyed coming up with ways for people to enjoy themselves, have fun with something I made. So we just keep going. Our apps brought in enough to fund our projects and pay the bills, and we lived pretty modestly anyway. It seemed like we just kept expanding and creating and somehow it was like the company grew overnight. Next thing we knew, we were working hand in hand with these large companies, helping their creative teams come up with ideas for new products."

"Okay," she started, "why is that such a big secret? Why is all of this such a big secret?" She gestured around the room. "Getting to 'play' for a living sounds pretty awesome. I feel like I'm still missing a piece of the puzzle?"

I didn't sense any underlying insults lurking in her words, or any sound of judgment. That was enough to encourage me to keep going. Taking a deep breath and finally relaxing my shoulders, I went for broke.

"It is pretty awesome, at least I thought so at first. Maybe you can't tell by looking at me now, but I was pretty nerdy in school. And I mean, your typical cliché nerd. Thick glasses, spent weekends playing D&D with my friends instead of going to parties, didn't even have my first kiss until I was 19. So when the people around me got wind of my growing success, my life really changed. All of a sudden I had more friends than I had time for, and there were girls throwing themselves at me. Honestly, I hated it. I knew they were only making the effort because of my success, but it was still nice not feeling so lonely all the time. I was too uncomfortable to give the women any attention, I couldn't even look girls in the eye, let alone spend any amount of time with one. Then one day Maggie came along, and that's when my life really changed."

"I see. So this is all about a girl." It disappeared as fast as it came, but I didn't miss that look of disappointment on her face. Was she disappointed because she was judging me for letting a girl affect me so much, or was it possible it was more out of jealousy? As much as I hoped it was the latter, I couldn't get ahead of myself. Before I lost my nerve, I turned to face her, ready to bare my soul to someone who was virtually a stranger to me still.

"Yes, it's about a girl. I'd love to be able to stand in front of you now and pretend that who I am is who I've always been, but truthfully, it's not even who I really am now. This confident, polished man in front of you is just an act. I learned quickly that people don't really care about who you really are. If you let people get too close to you, they will use your weaknesses against you. After Maggie, I never let anyone else in. Anyone other than those who already knew me, anyway. I learned how to play the part, be who I needed to be to maintain a safe distance from everyone around me."

"I guess I don't understand. Why is who you are so bad? What did Maggie do? I don't get why you have to hide all this in order to be whatever you think everyone wants you to be."

Immediately I wanted to close up, but I couldn't stop now. The look on her face was confusion, but the tone in her voice was soft. She was genuinely interested in finding out about me, and it was refreshing. Invigorating. Opening up was easier than I had thought it would be.

"Maggie and I started dating towards the very beginning. As the business grew, so did the expectations of everyone around me to 'act the part' of being a successful business owner. Suddenly, this shy, nerdy guy I'd always been wasn't good enough. Maggie would tell me over and over that I needed to 'grow up' and 'ditch the t-shirts' and 'start acting like a man and quit fooling around with toys.' I should have stood up for myself, argued with her. Who I was is what had made the company successful to begin with. But I thought I loved her, and I wanted to make her happy. So I let her change everything about me, mold me into who she wanted me to be. I was her puppet, and I completely lost myself during my relationship with her."

"So what happened? Where is Maggie now?"

"After 3 years of putting up with her, the demands, the insults...." My sentence trailed off. Here came the humiliating part. "I took her to a big charity event. There were going to be all sorts of famous people there and she was so excited. She actually managed to go an entire week without insulting me. I thought maybe things were getting better, that she was changing, finally noticing everything I had sacrificed for her. Anyway, I was mingling, chatting with some potential investors and she said she was going to get a drink. An hour later, she still hadn't returned so I went looking for her. I searched for almost thirty minutes, and when I couldn't find her, I went back to our limo to ask the driver if he had seen her, thinking maybe she had been ill and asked to go home. I don't know how, but I could just tell by the look on his face that I didn't want the answer to that question."

Adalyn inched even closer to me, removing her hand and instead twisting her arm around mine, then she leaned her head on my shoulder. Her smell, the feel of her, it was enough to instantly calm me and gave me the strength to keep going.

"The driver motioned with his head to the back of the limo. It was then that I noticed the motion, the limo was rocking slightly. So I opened the door and was faced with Maggie sitting on....some guys lap, completely naked, riding him with her head thrown back, screaming in pleasure. She didn't notice me at first, but the worst part was, when she finally did notice me, she didn't even look guilty. She didn't panic and start apologizing or trying to explain. She yelled at me. She called me a loser and started to call me more names but didn't finish because her orgasm broke through. I stood there, saying nothing, watching my girlfriend of four years having an orgasm on top of another guy inside of my limo. It was like I was frozen. I wanted to yell at her, pull that guy out and punch him, run away, anything. Instead, I stood there, and after the guy shot his load into her, she turned to me with a smirk on her face. Like she was pleased with herself."

"I'm so sorry, Ian. That's horrible. She seriously sounds like a bitch, and I can't even imagine what that was like. But you should know..." She wrapped her arms around my neck and took a deep breath, looking me directly in the eye. "Who you *really* are sounds pretty amazing to me." Slowly and gently she leaned up and put her lips on mine, and it was in that moment that I realized that as ridiculous as it sounded, I was already falling for this girl.

Before I could kiss her back, she pulled away and took off running, laughing as she looked back at me with a dare in her eyes.

"Where are you going?" I called out to her.

"To play!" She yelled back, smiling flirtatiously. "What do you say? Wanna have some fun with me?"

Shit. I wasn't falling for her. I already had.

CHAPTER 18

ADALYN

Falling down on my back, flushed and out of breath, I couldn't quit giggling. This was the most fun I'd had in ages. We'd been playing video games, jumping on trampolines, climbing rock walls and even played a full game of mini golf.

"I want to live here. Can I live here?" I asked, turning to smile at Ian who was laying next to me, not nearly as winded as I was.

"Ugh, why are you not as sweaty as me? You're barely winded," I teased, lightly punching his arm as I propped myself up on my elbow.

"I work out five days a week, plus I play in here a lot. You'd be surprised how in shape playing with toys all the time will make you." I hadn't laughed this much in my life. I really never wanted to leave. It had been the most amazing day.

I propped my head up in my hand, and really, truly looked at Ian for the first time. No assumptions or pre-judgments blocking my vision. Not looking for the worst, trying to find everything wrong with him that I could. Just looking at him, taking in what was before me. He really was beautiful.

Nodding at his shirt, I asked, "So what's the deal

with the t-shirt? Do you always wear your nerd clothes under your suit?"

He laughed and looked down at it. "When I was changing so much of myself, I was worried I would lose myself entirely and never be able to get it back. So yes, I always wear my 'nerd shirts' under my dress clothes. Even though no one can see it, I know they're there. It keeps me grounded, in a way."

"That's a shame, Kent."

"What is?" He looked at me questioningly.

"That you have to keep the best part of you hidden."

"My t-shirts?" He asked, laughing. "Most women think the best part of me is my handsome face and muscular body." His teasing wink made me grin.

"I'm not saying your good looks aren't a good quality to have, but they aren't your best feature. And sure, you have other things going for you too. You are smart, successful, charming. With everything I've found out about you today, it wouldn't surprise me to find you have superpowers, too. Can you fly, Kent? What else don't I know?"

"Why do you keep calling me Kent?"

"Seriously? You literally removed a suit to reveal a Superman shirt."

"Oh. So, like Clark Kent?"

"You know, for such a smart guy you're kind of dense," I laughed teasingly.

Suddenly he was on his feet and running out the door. I sat up, debating if I was supposed to follow him. Why had he ran out? Before I could decide what to do, he ran back in the room, wearing black, thick rimmed glasses. He came to a halt in front of me and puffed out his chest, putting his fists on his sides.

I was laughing hysterically. "Oh my gosh," I said trying to catch my breath between laughs. "You seriously are Clark Kent!"

He scooped me up in his arms and carried me towards the door. "Come on, Miss Lane. We have a job proposal to discuss."

And for the first time in five years, it didn't terrify me being held this way. It felt…perfect.

Ian sat me down in a chair in front of his desk. His office was a lot more formal in comparison to the rest of what I'd seen, but it was still in keeping with the theme of the place.

"I don't really do a lot of the business side of things in here. The next level down is where the formal business is conducted. If a client wants a meeting, if proposals need to be made, that all happens down there. I don't like to mix the business side of things with what we actually do," he said as he sat down behind his desk.

His desk was littered with trinkets. Bobble heads

and figurines, rubix cubes, and a few pictures of him with celebrities.

"Is this Leonard Nemoy?"

His cheeks flushed and the most adorable smile appeared. "Yeah, I met him last year at a comic book convention. We all go as a team to a lot of those types of events. Some of the most creative minds work in the entertainment industry. There is a lot to be learned from them. I guess you'll find out soon enough that we're all just a bunch of nerds, but we have a good time."

"Wow, that's amazing. I'm no trekkie, but I'm a huge Big Bang Theory fan. I kind of have a thing for nerds," I said with a shrug, placing the frame back on his desk. When I looked up at him he had one eyebrow raised in question. "What? Smart guys are hot, and I appreciate passion. 'Nerds' get a bad rap because a lot of what they are passionate about isn't considered trendy, but I think it's cool. You know, the definition of a 'nerd' is 'a foolish or contemptible person who lacks social skills or is boringly studious.' I don't think that definition holds true any more, they really should change it. Being a nerd shouldn't be an insult. I think loving something that doesn't make you 'popular' is brave. I wish I had something I was that passionate about, even if it was just a TV series or something. I guess I admire that in people. The devotion aspect of it all. People are just intimidated by those who are smarter and more confident in themselves. I mean, yeah, it seems like 'nerds' don't have social skills, but it's only because they know people are assholes so they avoid them. But they really don't care. If they did, they would stop liking all the things they do and start trying to fit in like the rest of the superficial, shallow idiots in the world. So I don't know…'nerds' are kinda awesome."

It was my turn to blush when I saw the look he was giving me when I finally stopped ranting. I looked away immediately, trying to convince myself that he wasn't looking at me like he wanted to leap across his desk and devour me.

He cleared his throat and sat up straighter, folding his hands together on top of his desk. "We can work out the exact details of your position on Monday. I'll need to give my lawyers a few days to draw up the contracts. As I told you before, normally we have all of that taken care of before we ever offer someone the position, so we are working a little out of order here. I just need to know what you are looking for in terms of compensation."

"Oh, well, I don't know. I mean, I'm just grateful to have a job. Especially somewhere as amazing as this. I don't need much to get by and I'm not really in a place to be making demands. If I can manage to get enough money in my bank account to replace my phone and buy some groceries then that's about all I'll need. So, really, just whatever you think I'm qualified to earn here I guess.

I still don't even know what I'll be doing here, or what I even have to offer. Unless you really want me to scrub the toilets. Which, honestly, at this point I would do," I shrugged, and fidgeted with my hands. I'd been rambling nervously and revealing way too much information.

"Oh, well, easy enough then. Starting pay is sixty thousand a year, our employees get paid salary. Also, you won't need to worry about replacing your phone. The company provides a phone to each of its employees and it can be used for personal use. The account will be paid for but will be in your name. It's part of your sign-on bonus. When we finalize things on Monday, once the contracts are signed, you'll get your sign-on bonus of five thousand. So assuming those amounts are adequate, then we can work out the rest of the details on Monday."

I about fell out of my chair. Holy snacks! That was more money that I'd ever made at any job. Then with the phone and sign-on bonus, I literally didn't know what to say. I was stunned into silence. Immediately I felt uncomfortable. There was no way I had anything to offer this company that would be worth what he was offering me.

"Wow, Ian, that's very generous of you but there is no way I can accept all of that. I still don't know what you have me doing here, but regardless, I can guarantee I'm not qualified for anything that would justify my being paid that much. I…I can't accept all of that. You should start me off lower. Let me prove myself first.. That way it's fair."

"Nonsense, Adalyn. If you are to be an employee here then you will receive the same benefits as everyone else. I'm afraid that's a deal breaker. I have to say though," he said with a smirk on his face, "you are the first employee who's ever asked for a pay decrease. Normally I'd have people trying to negotiate for more, yet before you even start you're trying to take less. You never cease to amaze me."

"I do have one stipulation in regards to the job, and it's non-negotiable."

"Name it."

"I can't work Friday afternoons. Every Friday from noon to four I need off. And I can't tell you why, you just have to trust it's important."

"Done." I sighed a breath of relief at Ian agreeing to giving me Friday afternoons off.

I still didn't feel comfortable making that much money, but maybe once I found out more details about what I would be doing it would help. No sense in arguing over it now. If I needed to put my foot down and demand less pay, I could do that on Monday. Only my dumb ass self would be asking for less money. I couldn't help it though. If I didn't deserve it, I didn't want it.

CHAPTER 19

IAN

After finalizing our plan to meet Monday morning, I walked Adalyn to the elevators. I had to keep reminding myself that this was an interview, not a date. I wanted so badly to pull her to me and kiss her deeply, but not only would that be unprofessional, but I was pretty sure she would slap me.

Still, I had made progress today. Never in a million years could I have imagined her reaction to everything about my work and my past that I had just dumped on her. She didn't mock me, didn't look at me like I was a loser. She didn't even look at me with pity when I told her about Maggie. She looked…understanding. Empathetic. Everything about her softened and it was clear that our relationship was now heading down a different path.

It would be hard remaining professional. I wanted Adalyn so badly. In my life, in my arms, in my bed. But I was a realistic man, and I knew it would take time to get Adalyn to finally see me as someone she could truly be herself with. Hopefully all the hours we would spend together at work would only help our relationship grow. I would just have to be careful not to cross any boundaries at work. I couldn't undo all the progress we'd made by further complicating things.

As the elevator doors closed, I turned on my heel and rushed back to my office. A lot had to happen before Monday. I needed to speak with the team about the new addition, had to have the lawyers working on the contracts, and I needed to get her a phone.

I couldn't tell you why in that moment I had told her so many lies. Well, not lies per se. Just not full truths. Not the same. Not really, anyway. Okay, kind of, but what's done is done.

So, no, not all employees got company phones in their own name. None of them got phones, period. And no, we don't generally give sign-on bonuses to every new hire. That's traditionally only given when we are acquiring someone with a unique talent that we desperately need for a project. And no, the starting pay is not sixty thousand. Well, it could be depending on what your position is, but since I had hired her for a non-existent position then the starting salary wasn't necessarily on par with everyone else's.

Why had I hired her for a position that didn't exist and given all these extra perks? I didn't know. I supposed I should ask my dick. I mean, my heart was definitely involved in the decision, but being near her and seeing that different side of her definitely caused the guy downstairs to start speaking his mind about things.

Yeah, I could be patient and try to win her over

without having to bribe her with a job to spend time with me. But she was consuming all my thoughts, I couldn't concentrate on anything. Maybe having her near me constantly would keep my mind from drifting so much.

Not likely, but worth a shot.

Plus, she really needed a job. It was my nature to help people. It would be the first time I hired an employee for an imaginary job just to help them, but it would work out. Adalyn really was talented. I didn't know why she hadn't gone to school for the arts. She was phenomenal, and with a little guidance, she could really flourish and become an exceptional employee. Whatever she needed, I would give her.

Somewhere, the radical part of my brain was freaking out. You don't build a successful company by making rash decisions over a girl. Even when Maggie was controlling every aspect of my life, she never controlled my work. She had never even been to my "real" office on the top floor. I didn't want her complaining and constant judgmental remarks bringing down the atmosphere.

Adalyn was different, though. Today was the first day in, I didn't even know how many years, that I actually felt comfortable truly being myself. I needed that. I needed to be able to feel that way more. And maybe all my motives for helping her sounded selfish, but there probably wasn't much I wouldn't do for this girl already. As scary as that was, it was the truth. She had me spellbound, and I didn't want it any other way.

Carrie came storming into my office early the next day looking pissed. Apparently word had gotten around about Adalyn coming to join us. I knew this would be an issue for her, but she would just have to get over it. I loved my baby sister, but she had a flare for the dramatic.

"What the hell, E!" She was standing right in front of my desk, hands on her hips, struggling for a breath. A light sheen of sweat was forming on her forehead and her hair was falling out of her ponytail. Long story short, she was a hot mess.

"You okay, Sis? You look…disheveled."

"Screw you, I was working on the choreography for yet another stupid dance game," she said as she tried to catch her breath. "That's not the point! You hired Adalyn? Are you freaking kidding me Ian?"

I stood up from my desk and walked around to her, putting my hands on her shoulders. She was over a foot shorter than me, being as I was six foot four and she was five foot three. I had to bend my knees to look her in the eye.

"I know you don't like Adalyn, but you're going to have to get over it. There really is no reason for you to dislike her. You're going to have to figure out one of these days how to deal with people you feel threatened by without lashing out at them."

She shrugged my arms away from her and took a step back.

"Don't, Ian. You know why I'm like this, you know I'm working on it. I was just staying away from her and I was dealing, but now I'm going to have to be around her every damn day! And I see the way you look at her. I know you think you feel something for her, but you need to be careful. I have a bad feeling about her and I just don't want you to get hurt."

"Carrie, you have nothing to worry about. I know what I'm doing. Adalyn is really talented and she's going to fit in great here. My personal feelings aside, bringing her on is a good decision. You just need to get to know her. Just give it a chance."

Carrie crossed her arms and started full on pouting. Temper Tantrum Carrie was the worst. Once she started acting like a toddler there was no reasoning with her. You just had to wait it out.

"Just go, Carrie. I'm not doing this right now. I don't have to justify my decisions for my business with you. I appreciate you looking out for me, but nothing you say is going to change anything. It's just going to start an argument and I hate fighting with you. Please, for everyone's sakes, just find a way to deal."

"Fine," she puffed, making a beeline for my door. "But when she screws something up or breaks your heart, I'll be there to help you pick up the pieces again like with Maggie, but you bet your ass I'll be saying I told you so." She started to leave, but stopped mid-stride, not bothering to turn around to face me this time. "Just be careful, E, that's all I'm asking," she muttered as she disappeared out of the room.

Carrie had been the one to help me get my sanity back after things went down with Maggie, even despite how much the situation affected her as well. If anything, what happened with Maggie was more detrimental to her than me. But Carrie stood strong and no one understood better than her the exact reasons why what happened with Maggie had caused such a blow to my confidence. I'd been shoved in lockers and had my face forced into toilet bowls growing up, but nothing made me feel like more of a loser than seeing Maggie's face as she rode some other guy's cock. I hit an all time low, didn't get out of bed for a week. I was such a pussy. There wasn't one insult you can throw at me about how I acted during and after my relationship with Maggie that I hadn't already said to myself.

It was a wake up call of epic proportions. I was a coward. I'd been hiding behind Maggie's controlling bitchiness, using it as an excuse to not really put myself out there. I hated Maggie, but I hated myself more. So while I was laying in bed feeling sorry for myself, Carrie was the one packing up Maggie's shit and throwing it out the window.

Literally. She threw anything Maggie had at my place out of the window of my apartment. Which was on the tenth floor. And it was raining.

The hysterical part of all of that is the bill I got in the mail from Maggie, demanding I pay her to replace all of the items of hers that Carrie ruined. I knew Maggie wouldn't relent until I gave in to her absurd demand for repayment, so I had intended to just pay her and sever all ties. Carrie had other plans.

As I was picking up the phone to call my banker and have a check issued, Carrie grabbed my phone and informed me she had taken care of it already. Apparently, she had gone to Maggie and told her that the limo had video cameras in it and there was video of her debauchery. I'm fairly certain Maggie had to have known she was lying, but apparently she didn't want to take the risk.

That was the last time I let my baby sister fight my battles for me. I loved her more than anything, but I'd been living so ass backwards for so long, it was time to man up. It took time and more pep talks with the mirror than I cared to admit, but I finally became someone I could be comfortable with. The only problem was, something was still missing.

I really thought I had overcome all the damage Maggie had inflicted. Although, to be fair, a lot of my self esteem issues started way before her. Being picked on your whole life does that to you. But I had managed to continue to grow my company and had become quite the 'ladies man' so to speak. I was no man whore, but I didn't go long without a companion in the bedroom. I had a few close friends whom I shared a mutual agreement with of the no-strings-attached variety and everything seemed to be perfect.

Until Adalyn. Until I spent the day with her yesterday, having more fun than I'd had in years. In that moment that she placed my face in her hands and looked at me with so much understanding and compassion, that's when I realized that I was only kidding myself. I was still playing a part. Just pretending. Every time I looked in her eyes it gave me more clarity as to what I needed to do, the reality I needed to face. I was done pretending and I wasn't going to hide myself or my feelings any longer.

Soon, very soon, Adalyn would see just how great we would be together. And the best part, was I knew once that happened, she would be with me. The real me. And with that thought, I took a deep breath and accepted that my life would never be the same.

CHAPTER 20

ADALYN

I knew the lines had been blurred at my interview. Part of me still worried that he had only given me the job because of Stacy or because he thought he had some sort of feelings for me. But honestly, at this point, I was desperate. For the job, not Ian. Just to clarify.

"Ugh, Stacy, I don't know what to wear!"

Stacy strolled casually into my bedroom wearing nothing but a pair of panties.

"Jesus, Stacy, get some clothes on. I love you, but I do not want to see you naked." I threw my robe at her while I held my other hand over my eyes.

"Oh my gosh, Addy. We have the same parts. It's nothing you haven't seen."

"Don't remind me. If I ever walk in on you on top of some guy on our couch again, I swear I'll move out. I'll sleep on a bench on the street with homeless people. I am scarred for life now."

Stacy just chuckled as she threw one of my t-shirts over her head. That girl had no concept of modesty.

"Just wear whatever, Ad. You said it's totally relaxed there right? Everyone was wearing jeans and dressed down. So dress like you normally do."

"It just feels wrong. This is my first day at my new

job. It's weird showing up looking like a bum."

"Aha! So you admit you dress like a bum!" I glared at her and threw a shoe at her head. "Hey! Don't get mad at me. I didn't buy your wardrobe. You have way more casual clothes than dressy ones. You should feel way more at ease in your everyday stuff."

I sighed. She's right. I never cared this much about what people thought. In fact, my usual M.O. would be to show up wearing the opposite of what I was supposed to. Coz you know, I was a rebel like that. Or maybe just immature. Eh, semantics.

"I am not looking forward to working with Carrie," I groaned as I pulled a light pink tank over my head. I pulled on a pair of skinny jeans and threw a pink and blue plaid shirt on over my tank, then slipped on my knee high boots.

"She's really not that bad once you get to know her, Ad. She's just got…issues. She means well, it's just hard for her to open up to people. Just be patient and give it time. Plus, she doesn't work there full time, she just does consulting so you probably won't see her very often."

"Stacy, you are the queen of bitchy comments and making things awkward. I cannot believe you are lecturing me on how to behave with someone. If this conversation were reversed, you'd be telling me to go fuck myself."

"Okay, fine, you're right. Do whatever you want.

But she is my friend, she's Ian sister and you're going to have to work with her. So if you don't want things to be super awkward and tense around her all the time, then you should probably take my suggestions."

Ugh, I hated when Stacy was being rational. If only she listened to her own advice once in a while her life might be a little less dramatic. But hell, Stacy would go stir crazy without drama. An idle Stacy is a crazy Stacy.

"Alright, I'm out of here. I'm already cutting it close. I don't want to be late on my first day. Although," I said, spinning around on my heel, turning back to my bedroom. "Maybe I should pack an extra set of clothes in case what I'm wearing is stupid. I don't want to be stuck in this outfit all day if it's going to make me uncomfortable."

"Oh my gosh, get out!" Stacy yelled, shoving me towards the door. "You'll be fine, you look hot. In a cowgirl, virgin-esque kind of way. Just go or you'll be late."

"Okay, fine. I'll text you later."

"You know," Stacy yelled down the hallway as I made my way towards the elevators. "If you threw your hair up in some pigtails and got a cowboy hat, I bet you could live out one of Ian's fantasies over his desk!"

I swear, all Stacy ever thought about was sex. I couldn't help but smile at the idea though. *Stop it, Addy! Don't go there!* Shaking my head and forcing the aching feeling in my nether regions at the thought of Ian bend-ing me over his desk, I pushed the button and sat back against the wall. Avoiding the temptation of Ian's sexy body was going to be exhausting. I hoped I had time to grab some coffee.

The first two weeks flew by. I felt like all I ever did was socialize, but everyone assured me that it was important that we all know each other really well in order to work cohesively. I was still in training, so I mostly just did little tasks that were given to me by different team members, though they always asked me and phrased it as me doing them a favor. I knew they were just trying to make me comfortable and not come across as bossy. I appreciated their forethought.

Currently I was working on designing the packaging for a new water bottle the team had designed. It was my first real shot at doing something completely on my own, without having direction from someone else. I was given full reign on the design and it was stressing me out. Badly. Normally the pressure to do well would break me, but I wanted to prove myself. Instead of being afraid of failure, I was motivated to succeed.

It was strange. I felt…grown up. Don't get me wrong, I struggled with this constantly. I went back and forth with myself, fighting the urge to cower and run. I didn't want to mess this up. I wanted to be responsible for once and show Ian that I was worth the risk I knew he took on me.

He had no reason to trust me with this. Yeah, sure, he'd seen some of my sketches and paintings I'd done, but they wouldn't be hanging in the Louvre anytime soon. I always had the creative gene and once I put my mind to something, I generally would accomplish it and be proud of the results. The issue with that is that I only ever worked on projects that I actually wanted to do. It didn't matter how exciting or fun it might have been, if I was being told to do it, I just simply wouldn't.

This made my school age years extremely challenging for my parents. Luckily, my mom was very similar and was very patient with my stubbornness. Unfortunately, my teachers were a lot less understanding. I ended up doing a lot of extra homework to try and raise my grades after they inevitably plummeted from my refusing to cooperate.

Medial, mundane tasks weren't the issue. Your standard, run-of-the-mill types of assignments were a piece of cake. It was the assignments that required me to think outside the box, put a little of myself into them and chance the possibility of failing that really did me in. My fear of failure was a great hindrance in my life and I wish I could tell you where it stems from, but probably only a trained professional would be able to decipher my crazy lack of self esteem.

Again, only with the things that actually mattered to me. In what ways did it hinder me, you ask? I think the better question would be in what ways *didn't* it hinder me. All those school musicals I wanted so badly to be a part of? I just sat in the audience watching them. Having to audition was too terrifying. Not because I didn't believe I was good enough. I was probably even a little full of myself when it came to some of my talents, but that wasn't the point. Just because you are good at something doesn't mean you won't fail.

School wasn't the only aspect of my life that suffered from this. My social life was a joke. All the boys who I actually found interesting and attractive were the ones I avoided. Several of them even tried to ask me out. I should have been excited, right? Well, I wasn't. I was terrified. And when I get scared, I get cruel. So after laughing at a few of them after they attempted to date me, they quit asking.

That didn't keep me from dating. Nope, I just had a tendency to date guys I had absolutely no interest in. Didn't matter if they were boring or ugly or stupid, it only mattered that they meant nothing to me. They couldn't hurt me if they meant nothing.

The same went when it came to having friends. Girls play head games. They are cruel and vicious and I had no desire to be a victim to the crap that went down between two girl friends.

No, I wasn't a loner. I had friends, but the same concept as dating applied. They were boring and homely looking, not even the least bit interesting. But they were kind and weren't judgmental and I knew they wouldn't turn on me just because one of the popular girls started talking to them. Because the popular girls didn't even look at them. It was hard to see them with their noses so high up in the air.

I never really fit in anywhere. I just kind of...existed. No one picked on me, and once my senior year of high school came, everyone had lost interest in me entirely.

Now, it wasn't like I walked around feeling sorry for myself. I didn't hang my head in shame or avoid eye contact. I was perfectly happy with how things were in my life. I was pretty and smart and probably could have fit in just about anywhere if I had actually cared enough to try, but I didn't. It wasn't worth all the effort. Everyone who purposely 'fit in' with a certain crowd had to constantly work at it. I simply didn't care enough to live every second of my life trying to make someone else happy, just to end up getting hurt in the long run.

So anyway, here I was at eleven o'clock on a Friday night, tossing dozens of wadded up sketches into the trashcan. I was determined not to leave this place until I had something I was happy with. I only had a week to come up with an idea to pitch to Ian, and if he liked it, we would pitch it to the sister company who was making the bottles.

I decided I need a break. Some caffeine, preferably. So I grabbed my drawing pad and slipped my flats back on to my feet and headed out to the kitchen in the break room. There were generally still several other employees here at this time of night, even on a Friday, but they were all out at some convention. I had decided not to go, wanting to take the opportunity of uninterrupted time to focus on my sketches.

As I grabbed a Red Bull and went to close the fridge, Ian's face appeared, inches from mine.

"Holy shit, Ian, you scared me."

Chapter 21

Ian

"Sorry, I didn't mean to sneak up on you. I didn't realize anyone was still here."

I reached down and picked up her sketch pad that she dropped when I startled her.

"What's this?" I asked, gesturing at the page that had fell open with the book.

"Ummm…that's just a doodle. I haven't been happy with anything I've drafted yet and sometimes when my mind wanders I just doodle. I honestly don't even remember drawing that," she chuckled as she took the sketch pad out of my hands.

"Well your doodles are amazing. Instead of calling them doodles you should probably call them masterpieces."

Her blush was adorable. I'd been trying to give her space since she started, letting her get acclimated and get to know everyone. Standing this close to her, looking at her beautiful face, I had to wonder what the hell had given me the bright idea to stay away.

"It's getting late. Are you planning on leaving soon?" I was probably here for the night, trying to meet a deadline for a new client. I secretly hoped Adalyn would say she's staying longer. Just knowing she's somewhere near me, even if I can't see her, made my body and mind more relaxed.

"I don't know. I was actually thinking of making some popcorn and watching a movie in the theater room. I'm too wired to relax right now, but I need to get my mind off this project for a bit. Is that okay?" She was looking down and fidgeting with her hands. I'd noticed she did that when she was nervous. Every time I saw her doing it, it took everything in me not to put my hands over hers to calm her.

"You don't have to ask my permission to do any-thing here, Adalyn. Consider this your second home. There are no rules here." She just nodded, mumbling an apology. This shy, insecure version of her was a sight to be seen. As much as I hated her doubting herself like this, and as much as I loved strong, confident Adalyn, I couldn't help my fascination. I found myself wondering how many people had been witness to this side of her. I also found myself hoping that it hadn't been very many. That I was special to her in some way.

"Okay, great, well...I guess I'll head over there. Have a good night," she said as she waved awkwardly. I had to bite my lip to keep from grinning at her obvious discomfort. "Unless…"

"Unless, what?"

"Unless…you want to watch a movie with me? I mean, I'm sure you're really busy. Never mind, of course you're busy. Plus it's late. Sorry, I don't know what I... anyway, have a good night."

She tried to run off, but I grabbed her by the elbow. I waited until she turned to look at me before I moved. Then in one swift step toward her, I brought my face inches from hers and looked into her dark, beautiful brown eyes. I heard her breath catch and her body stiffened. All I would have to do is lean a fraction in her direction and our mouths would touch. She was staring at my lips and I could tell she was anticipating me to do just that. So I leaned in close enough so that she could feel a ghost of my lips across hers, breathing into her parted lips as I whispered, "I'd love to watch a movie, but I get to pick it."

Then I took off running towards the theater, leaving a stunned Adalyn in the dust. Glancing back at her, I saw a slow smile creep across her face. And then she was running after me.

The theater room was essentially a small movie theater. Maybe like the quarter of the size of a normal one. There were three rows of plush, reclining chairs. Then a row of couches made of the same materials, and then another three rows of chairs. They were all extremely comfortable. I would know - I'd fallen asleep in them many times.

I wasn't tired tonight though. I had let Adalyn pick the seats since I got to pick the movie, and much to my surprise and delight, she had chosen one of the couches. We were sharing a bucket of popcorn, so despite the size of the couch, her body was right up next to mine.

"This movie is so stupid," she scoffed, right as one of the actors got massacred.

"What are you talking about? Quentin Tarantino is a genius. This movie is awesome."

"Some of his films are, but this one's just dumb," she laughed as I threw popcorn at her face. It caught in her hair and I leaned over to pull it out, letting my fingers linger a little longer than necessary, enjoying the softness of her long, dark hair.

The air between us seemed to thin and suddenly felt electrified. We had been joking at laughing at all the cheesy parts of the movie, completely relaxed, and I was truly enjoying myself. The moment was there again, she wanted me to kiss her. Her breathing picked up and she stared at my lips. I leaned toward her, easing my body against hers and she went with it, lowering her back to the couch.

When she was laying flat and I was hovering over her, I reached my hand towards her face and her eyes closed in anticipation of my touch. But I didn't stop, I kept going, and grabbed her sketch book off the seat. She opened her eyes, looking confused and surprised, as I sat up and started flipping through the book.

"Hey, those are private! You can't see those until I'm ready. Give it back."

Oh, this flirty, cat-and-mouse game we had going on was such a turn on. Knowing how much she wanted me to make a move only encouraged me to prolong the anticipation. I wanted to get her to the point of needing me so badly that she was begging. If I could hold on that long, because right now she was reaching her whole body against mine, reaching for the sketch pad I was holding above my head.

Yep, I was twelve again. I may as well pull her pigtails while I'm at it. I couldn't help it though. She was giggling and rubbing her stomach and breasts against me as she continue to grab for her drawings. It was a half assed effort, she could have grabbed it ten times by now. No, she was enjoying this as much as I was, and I was not about to stop her.

I lost my balance and fell back a little and her body moved with mine, causing her to be practically on top of me. Her eyes went dark and I felt my pants tighten from my arousal. I saw the moment she felt it, a myriad of emotions crossed her face and she pulled away quickly. She cleared her throat and mumbled something about using the restroom.

Sitting up, running my hands through my hair, I was mentally kicking myself for not kissing her when I had the chance. I just hoped I would get another opportunity. And soon.

Adalyn never came back to the theater. I waited thirty minutes before I went looking for her. I found her huddled in a far corner of the break room, her knees pulled up to her chest as she looked far off, lost in thought. As I approached her she looked up to me, and I could see her body shaking slightly as if she were on the verge of crying.

I sat down next to her and placed my hand gently on her knee. "What's wrong, Adalyn?" I said a silent prayer in that moment that this wasn't because of our flirting. The thought of her closing up on me again made my chest tighten.

"I just don't want to mess up, Ian," she whispered as she looked away. I pulled her chin up to face me so I could look in her eyes, my confusion apparent. "I…I'm happy here. I actually really want to be here. I want to do well. For the first time in maybe my entire life, I actually want to try and it scares me to death. I just…I don't want to mess up."

And I knew what she was talking about. She wasn't talking about the job, she was talking about me. About us. Whatever was happening between us, she felt it too, and she was afraid it would jeopardize her job here.

I could have assured her that it wouldn't. I could have pleaded with her to trust me and to not fight the inevitable, but words didn't go far with Adalyn. I had learned that the hard way. No, the only way to get through to her would be to give her space as she needed it and show her that I wasn't going anywhere. That she could feel safe here. With her job, and with me.

So as much as it pained me to do so, I pulled my hand away from hers and nodded. "I understand, Adalyn. I think you're doing great and you will go far with this company. I appreciate your dedication and I'll let you get back to it. Have a great night," I said, giving her a tight smile. It was forced and not at all believable, but the effort I was making didn't go unnoticed. She returned my smile with a forced smile of her own, and I couldn't help but notice her body relax the further I got from her. All the way to my office I tried to convince myself that it wasn't killing me that distance was what she needed from me.

No, that didn't hurt at all.

CHAPTER 22

ADALYN

The next few weeks of work passed in pretty much the same fashion as the first two. I didn't see much of Ian after that night. The night of the movie. Of the almost kisses. Of the long, focused gazes into each other's eyes. You know…that night.

He was giving me space. He had understood what I was asking of him loud and clear, without me having to voice it, and I would be eternally grateful to him for that. Ian had been more than respectful since the day I'd met him, so why did I feel so disappointed from him giving me what I wanted?

It was what I wanted, wasn't it? Yes, it's what I wanted. What I needed. For the first time in my life I was enjoying my job, giving it my all and actually succeeding. I couldn't jeopardize that just to satisfy my sexual urges. Even without my job being a complication, there was also the matter of him being Stacy's friend. No matter how I played out the situation in my head, sleeping with Ian would ultimately be a mistake.

Especially considering the fact that my feelings were bordering on becoming more than just sexual.

He was so devastatingly sexy that when I was near him it was like my brain was completely clouded in a lust induced haze. But every so often, when the fog would lift and I could truly see the man before me, my heart would soften just a little bit more. Ian was gradually working his way into my life in ways I hadn't let anyone be a part of for a very long time. It was terrifying, but I couldn't deny how much I also desperately wanted that with him.

I wanted him to see me, to know me, to understand me. It was all more than I could dare to hope for, so as much as I wished I could have an intimate relationship with Ian, I had to accept it would never happen. It couldn't happen. I didn't have a choice.

Unfortunately, no matter how many times I told myself that, practically keeping it on loop in my head 24/7, it couldn't prevent all the things I shouldn't feel from rising up whenever he was near.

Tonight, especially, would be extraordinarily difficult.

Our company was hosting a large charity event. Ian had founded the charity, and it was to raise awareness to school bullying. Obviously, an issue near to his heart. His involvement in the organization was touching, as he didn't just donate money but also his time. I couldn't take my eyes off of him as he sat patiently at a table full of children, probably middle school aged. It was so bizarre seeing him in a tux, sitting so casually with a group of kids, listening intently as they rambled on excitedly. It was endearing, and I felt myself wanting to swoon.

Ugh, I've got it bad.

At that moment, Carrie entered my line of vision, glaring at me like I was something she had drug in on the bottom of her shoe. I'd been doing a fantastic job of avoiding her at work. The place was large enough and with no one having set work hours, running into her didn't happen often. When it did happen, she would just stare at me and grumble under her breath. Usually my entering a room was her cue to exit. Not tonight, apparently.

"What, Carrie? What do you want?" My feet were killing me in these ridiculously high stilettos, and I'd been in my gown for so long that I was desperately yearning for a pair of sweatpants. I'd grown so accustomed to dressing casually every day at work that having to dress this way tonight was even more uncomfortable than usual. Although, I had to admit that I looked pretty fantastic in my dress. The long, purple silk of my gown clung to my body in all the right places and the delicate beading that spanned the dress in a beautiful design sparkled under the lights. I felt a little bit like a princess.

"Quit staring at my brother."

That got my attention. "What?" I snapped at her. "First of all, I'm not staring at your brother. Second of all, maybe you should mind your own damn business."

She snorted at the same time as rolling her eyes. Is she seriously my age? She behaves more like she belongs over at that table with the rest of the kids.

"Deny it all you want, Adalyn, but I'm not blind. You're fooling yourself if you think anything will ever happen between the two of you."

"I'm not thinking anything of the sort, not that it's any of your business. And I'm pretty sure your brother is a grown ass man and can handle himself. Tell me, Carrie, how would Ian feel about you coming over here and spitting your hatefulness in my face on his behalf?"

Her face fell and the arms she'd had crossed over her chest fell slack to her sides. Her eyes widened just a fraction, then narrowed, returning to stone.

"Just stay away, Adalyn. I mean it."

Then she was gone. Good riddance. Even if I was thinking of trying to date Ian, his crazy sister would be enough to talk me out of it. But I wasn't thinking of dating him. Not at all. Nope.

Ugh, screw it, I needed a glass of wine. I hadn't driven, so what was the harm, right? Pretending to not have feelings for Ian was really wearing me down. I just needed a brief reprieve. As I approached the bar, Ian slid in next to me, sitting on a vacant stool.

"Is there something about my presence that leads you to drinking?" Ian teased, nudging my arm with his.

If only he knew just how true that was.

"I just don't do well in these situations, the dressing up and stuff atmosphere. It's not really my scene,"

I shrugged as I took a sip of the wine the bartender had just handed me.

"Yeah, me either. I was actually thinking of heading out and grabbing a bite to eat. The food here was disgusting and I'm starving." Ian scrunched up his nose and made a face over the food. He was so cute like this, I couldn't stop the giggle that escaped my lips. A real giggle. I was officially pathetic.

"That actually sounds great. Can we swing by the office first though? I've got a change of clothes there and I'm dying to get out of these shoes." Ian stood and placed his hand on the small of my back. I pretended to not notice the flutters it was causing in my stomach. I didn't miss, however, the glare coming from Carrie as we headed towards the door. So I winked. I couldn't help myself, she just got under my skin.

To my surprise, Ian had driven himself. I had expected him to ride in a limo or some extravagant town car. In the least, I thought he would be driving an Aston Martin or some other ridiculously expensive car. Instead, he was driving an old trans am. It was in great condition, but it wasn't at all what I would picture Ian driving. I had to admit that he looked sexy in his tux driving a vintage car though.

The ride to the office and up the elevators to our

floor was filled with comfortable small talk and laughter. Ian was so easy to talk to and was such a great listener. The more time we spent together, the more difficult it became to deny the feelings I was having towards him. The sexual attraction had always been there, but those feelings were never hard for me to ignore. The constant urge to hold his hand, reach out and touch his face or just lean into his body with my head on his chest…those feelings were impossible to ignore. They were so foreign that I didn't even know how to begin fighting them.

When the elevators opened to our floor, Ian and I were still laughing over a story he was telling about the time he hacked into the school's database and got the answers to a test, when we heard muffled sounds coming from down the hall. It wouldn't be unusual for someone to be working at this time of night, even on a weekend, but the sounds definitely did not sound normal.

We cautiously made our way down the hall, and as we heard the whispers and muffled sounds, I became increasingly nervous. Were there intruders in the building? A million different scenarios started running through my head and I instinctively reached for Ian's hand. All of a sudden the muffled sounds became clearer and we heard someone shriek out a loud cry. Before I could even process what just happened, Ian was already running. Full on sprinting towards the source of the commotion.

I took off after him and turned the corner just in

time to see Ian pull Martin, one of our team members, off of Lily, one of our developers. Ian grabbed Martin by the neck with one hand and slammed him down on the ground. Lily cried out, pulling my attention from Martin struggling to get out of Ian's grip, and I ran over to her. I hugged her tightly, trying to soothe her, and led her towards the door. I glanced over my shoulder just in time to see Ian land a punch directly to Martin's jaw, causing blood to spurt out of his mouth.

Lily and I walked out to the break room and she sat on a couch while I made her a cup of tea. I knew too well what was happening in there. Her shirt was torn, her face streaked with the constant flow of tears, and her right eye was already red and starting to swell. The only consolation to all of this is that she was still clothed, so maybe he hadn't hurt her. At least, not in that way.

Lily was still sobbing uncontrollably when the police arrived. As the officers escorted Martin out of the building, a paramedic approached Lily, checking her for injuries. I offered several times to ride with her to the hospital, but Lily had insisted she would be fine and that her sister was meeting her there. I didn't want her to feel alone, but the humiliation of what I'd witnessed was obvious on her face and I didn't want to make her any more uncomfortable. She had absolutely nothing to be ashamed of, and I resolved that I would give Lily a few days, but then I was going to try to talk to her about what happened. I was confident I could help her.

Ian approached me as the last of all the emergency personnel exited our office and I sighed in exhaustion. It had been two hours since we arrived to find Lily and Martin, and despite my exhaustion and hunger from still not having had dinner, I was so incredibly grateful we had gotten here in time to prevent Martin from hurting Lily any more than he already had.

Looking over at Ian, you could see the exhaustion in his body as well, but in his eyes was anger. The way he had leapt into action with no second thought, instinctively protecting Lily - it was messing with my head. He ran a hand through his hair, his shirt half untucked and his clothes wrinkled from the struggle. He looked disheveled and perfect. He gave me a tight smile when he saw me staring at him, and every reason I'd been telling myself to stay away from Ian just disappeared. So I wrapped my hands around his neck and roughly pulled his lips to mine.

CHAPTER 23

IAN

Adalyn was kissing me. No, Adalyn was consuming me. My adrenaline was still hot, coursing through my veins from the struggle with Martin, but my body's reaction to Adalyn's mouth on mine was feral. Primal. The need to have her close to me, to be inside of her, took over and I was no longer in control of my body.

I picked her up and she wrapped her legs around mine, our mouths never breaking contact. Her hands were all over me, exploring, searching. Our mouths continued their assault, and I held her tight as I led us down the hall to my office. As soon as we were inside the door, Adalyn pulled her mouth from mine and slid her body slowly down mine, then reached her hand behind her locking the door, never breaking eye contact.

She placed her hand on my chest, gently pushing me backwards toward the couch along the far wall of my office and I fell backwards as my knees made contact with the cushions. Adalyn climbed onto my lap, straddling my legs as she ran her index finger from my neck, moving slowly down my chest to the button on my pants.

"This is how this is going to happen," she said as she tugged on the waist of my pants, slipping her fingers inside and lightly grazing my stomach. "I am in control, I call the shots. No questions, no resisting. Can you handle that?" My silence and confusion caused her to still. She pulled her hand away and looked me directly in the eyes and asked again, "Can. You. Handle. That."

Under normal circumstances a beautiful woman taking charge in the bedroom, err, office, would be a turn on. But something in her eyes gave me pause. The desire was still there, but the Adalyn I had come to know was missing. Something vacant and distant had washed over her, and suddenly this seemed like a bad idea. I didn't want this Adalyn. I didn't want whatever facade she was giving me at that moment.

I slid my hands into hers and studied her face, trying to figure out where my Adalyn had gone. "Why are you doing this, Adalyn? Where did you go? This isn't you."

She forcefully pulled her hands from mine and jumped off of me, backing away and biting down on her lip to try and stop it from quivering, but it was too late. I knew I was right, something was different.

"Why are you doing this, Ian? Why can't you just do what I'm asking? I'm sure relinquishing control to a woman is something you're familiar with," she spat at me, with a hateful edge in her tone. I knew what she was implying. She was talking about Maggie. And yes, while Maggie was very controlling in every other aspect of my life, she was never controlling in the bedroom. Not that I would have minded.

"Control isn't the issue for me, Adalyn, and you know that. Mutual respect and honesty - that's what's important. And right now, you aren't being honest with me." I stood and approached her slowly, even as she continued to match my steps toward her with steps backward of her own. Once she met resistance with the wall she froze and her eyes widened just a fraction.

"What, Adalyn? Talk to me. I'll give you what you want, whatever it is you need. You need control? You can have it, it's yours. Just tell me why you need this, tell me why it's so important. Let me in, Adalyn," I said as I placed my palm over her heart, and brought my other hand up and gently brushed my thumb down her cheek and then over her bottom lip.

A sob escaped her before she could stop it, and the torture and sadness in her face stole my breath. She was in pain and I found myself getting angry. Not at her, but at whatever had caused such torment to this amazing woman that she couldn't bring herself to let me in. I needed to know. I had to know. Whatever was hurting her, I wouldn't be able to rest until I found a way to help her. Show her that I would never add to that pain.

"Just stop it, Ian! Stop!" She smacked my hand away and pushed off the wall, and I let her past, knowing she needed some distance in that moment. "I can't give you what you're asking. I can't be what you need. Why can't what I'm offering you be good enough?"

"Adalyn," her name left my mouth more like a plea, a begging question. "Please…"

I moved one step toward her, reaching my hand out, but she dropped her head. "I can't, Ian," she whispered, then she turned and walked out.

It took everything in me not to go after her. Not to lock her in here with me until I found a way to get through to her, but no one could make Adalyn do anything. She had proven that time and again. And when I finally got through to her, and I *would* get through to her, I wanted her to tell me because it's what she wanted. Not because I had pressured her or coerced her into it.

I didn't know when it had happened, at what point it became more than an attraction, but I was in love with Adalyn. Whatever secrets she was harboring, whatever pain she was suffering - she didn't deserve to be struggling with it all alone. I didn't know how yet, but I would find a way to show her that she could trust me. I wouldn't be able to rest until I did.

I hadn't seen Adalyn for six days. She hadn't come in to work during the day, but I knew she had been in because I was still getting daily updates via email regarding the progress on her project. I found myself staying later and later, hoping to run into her, but I couldn't bring myself to go looking for her. She needed space, and as much as it killed me to give it to her, I knew pressuring her to see me before she was ready would only hurt her even more.

I hadn't been sleeping. At least, not well, anyway. That night was haunting me. Part of me worried that I had made it worse by stopping her. I had the worst case of blue balls that I'd ever had in my entire life because I'd stopped her, but I did nothing to relieve the ache. I welcomed the pain, the discomfort, the distraction. Anything to pull attention away from the ache that was growing in my chest.

I missed her. Her company, her conversation - even her sarcasm. I worried constantly that I had ruined whatever was happening between us. That I had undone all the progress we had made and pushed her away. I feared she had taken my stopping her as rejection, as me not wanting her.

I did want her. More than I'd ever wanted anyone in my entire life. My body craved her, my need for her consumed me. I couldn't eat, couldn't focus. I hadn't gotten any work done all week. My body was so weak from exhaustion and not eating that I couldn't even work out. I was a pathetic mess, but I couldn't find a way to pull myself out of it.

When Friday rolled around, one week since that night, I decided I couldn't take it any more. I needed to see her, needed to know how she was doing. I stood up from my desk and walked towards her office. It was half past midnight and I had no idea if she was still here, but as soon as I walked into the break room I saw her. She was curled up on one of the couches, reading a book.

She looked beautiful. Her hair was pulled up into a messy bun on the top of her head, there were bags under her eyes, she didn't have a stitch of makeup on and she was wearing baggy sweat pants and an oversized t-shirt. And she was gorgeous. My heart started pounding in my chest at the sight of her, and I took a few deep breaths to slow it down before I approached her.

"Adalyn," I whispered, stopping in front of her. She didn't move for several seconds, and I wondered if she had even heard me, But then she slowly lifted her head to look at me and offered me a weak smile. That pain I had seen that night in my office was still there. It had never left. The time away from her hadn't helped her, she'd just been suffering alone.

"Adalyn, please…I just need to…" she reached her hand up, interrupting me, and pulled me down on to the couch next to her.

"Just sit with me, Ian. Please," she begged, her eyes already starting to mist over. "I don't want to talk, I just don't want to be alone. Will you just sit with me a while?"

I didn't respond. I just wrapped my arms around her and pulled her to me, and she leaned against my side, resting her head on my shoulder.

I don't know how long we sat like that. I felt a few tears that had rolled down her cheeks land on my arm, and I rubbed my hand up and down her arm and pulled her tighter. I held her while she quietly sobbed, and eventually her crying slowed along with her breathing, and she drifted off to sleep.

I felt my own exhaustion taking over, my eyes becoming heavy. Sitting there with Adalyn in my arms was the most relaxed I had been all week, and after a while I drifted off with her.

I startled awake, my eyes snapping open. I didn't know how late it was or how long I'd been asleep, but my arms were empty. Adalyn was gone, and I'd never felt more alone in my life.

CHAPTER 24

ADALYN

It had been damn near impossible to remove myself from Ian's embrace when I woke up, but as right as it felt being in his arms, I had to get out of there. I didn't let men comfort me. I didn't lay in their arms or fall asleep on their chest. I didn't let myself be in any kind of vulnerable position around a man, regardless of whether or not I wholly trusted that man.

And I did. Trust Ian, that is. As much as I told myself that I shouldn't, as much as I tried to convince myself that I was only kidding myself, I couldn't help it. Ian had done the impossible. He had made his way into my heart.

It didn't matter though. This wasn't about what I wanted or what I felt. Ian deserved better. He deserved someone who could care for him in a way I couldn't. He deserved someone to give all of them self to him, to be completely honest and a whole other slew of things I couldn't do.

As I opened the door to Stacy's apartment, doing what felt a hell of a lot like the walk of shame at three in the morning, I didn't expect to see Stacy sitting on the couch staring at me like she was about to kill me.

"What the hell, Stace? Why are you awake? And

why are you looking at me like I killed your cat?"

"First of all, I hate cats, so if I had one you'd have my blessing to kill it. They are evil. Second of all, we need to talk."

"Uhh...okayyyy? Can it wait until later? I'm exhausted and I really just want to go lay down."

"No, it can't wait until later. It's going to happen right now. And don't bother arguing with me, it's a waste of time. There's coffee in the kitchen, so you can stall long enough to make yourself a cup, but then you're sitting your ass down right here on this couch and talking to me."

Dammit. I already knew what this was about. I'd completely withdrawn since that night with Ian. I'd been avoiding her and everyone else, and when I did happen to cross paths with her, I avoided her like the plague. Stacy could read me better than anyone else and she would figure out quickly what was wrong and I wasn't ready to talk about it.

"Hurry up, Addy! It doesn't take that damn long to make a cup of coffee."

I groaned and made my way back into the living room. "Have you been to bed, Stacy? Why are you up?"

"No, I haven't been to bed. I've been patiently waiting for you to come home so I could force you to talk to me. You've been avoiding me, don't think I didn't notice. You can't keep things from me, Addy. I gave you some space, hoping futilely that you would come to me, but I should have known better. So enough's enough. Talk."

"I don't want to talk Stacy. I'm begging you not to make me. I promise I'll get over this and I'll go back to normal, just give me more time."

"Alright, that's it," she said as she tossed her arms up into the air. "You've obviously lost your damn mind." She scooted closer on the couch and I tried to move away but I was already up against the arm and couldn't move any further. "Quit pulling away, I'm hugging you. You're going to sit there and you're going to let me." She pulled me into a big bear hug and squeezed me so tight I thought I might suffocate. I held onto my anger and annoyance as long as I could, and then I gave up. I sobbed uncontrollably, full on ugly crying, while I told Stacy everything. Every detail of every moment since I'd met Ian.

"Finally," she said as she finally removed her tight hold on me. "Do you know how hard it's been for me to not bug the shit out of you the last two months? I knew something was going on with Ian. I didn't know what, but I thought he was getting through to you so I didn't push it. I didn't want to make waves when progress was being made. I'm glad to know I was right for once."

"What do you mean?"

"He did make progress. More than anyone else has

ever made. More than your therapists, counselors, me or your parents. He did it, Addy."

"Did what? What are you talking about?"

"He made you feel."

"The only thing he's made me feel is embarrassed and ashamed. I humiliated myself that night I threw myself at him, and I'm ashamed for all the pain I've been causing him. I know he's confused and hurt from my shutting him out, but it's how it has to be. He just has to accept that nothing will happen between us."

"Bullshit."

"Excuse me?"

"I said, bull. shit," she enunciated each word slowly as she narrowed her eyes at me. "You feel a hell of a whole lot more than shame and embarrassment. You care about him Addy, you're just trying to convince yourself you don't. And you're not doing a very good job either, because it's very obvious how you feel." I fought back the tears threatening, shaking my head and trying to find a way to argue with what she was saying.

I couldn't though. She was right. I did care about Ian. I cared about him so much that it was terrifying. More terrifying than anything I had ever experienced in life, and that's what made it so much worse. That's what solidified for me that I couldn't do anything about it, couldn't act on my feelings. I wasn't selfish enough to do that to Ian.

"I do care, Stacy. I'm done trying to convince my-self that I don't. But I'm scared. Not just scared, terri-fied. Not just of getting hurt, but of hurting him. He is just amazing, Stacy. So much more than I deserve." She started to argue and I held my finger up to her mouth to stop her. "I'm not saying I don't deserve happiness or love or whatever…but I don't deserve him. It's not me feeling sorry for myself, it's just the truth. Maybe if I wasn't still such a mess, I don't know, maybe I could be what he deserves. But I can't, Stacy. I'm just being real-istic. He thinks he cares about me but he doesn't know me, not really."

"Then tell him. Let him know you, Addy. You do deserve him. You deserve love and happiness as much as anyone else and Ian is a good guy. It's obvious he cares about you too."

"That's exactly why I can't tell him. He does care and he isn't just a good guy, he's great. There's a good chance that once he knows everything, he would feel too guilty to let me go out of obligation to help me or a feeble attempt to try and fix me. I don't want pity in a relationship. I don't want to be a project. I can't be in any kind of real relationship until I'm whole again so that I can fully give myself to someone."

"That's just your bullshit therapy crap talking. You're not broken, Addy. You're not a mess. You don't need fixed. Everyone has pain, okay? Everyone has things in life that they need to overcome, pasts and secrets and pain that we carry around. Yeah, yours is shittier than most, but that doesn't make you any less deserving than anyone else. A relationship means having someone to help carry your burdens, ease your pain. Needing someone doesn't make you weak, Adalyn."

Her words were too painful to hear. I knew they were true, I knew what she was saying made sense, but it just didn't apply to me. It couldn't. I had accepted a long time ago that things just weren't normal for me.

"Stop it, Adalyn," Stacy barked, pointing her finger in my face. "I know what you're thinking. Quit thinking that the normal rules don't apply to you. That because you've suffered something tragic that that somehow makes you different from the rest of the world. It does make you different from a lot of people. It makes you stronger, braver. You aren't going to hurt Ian by letting him in. You're hurting him now by keeping him out. Don't push him away Adalyn. Just take a chance. Not all risks are a mistake."

She was right. I hated when she was right. "Thank you, Stacy," I said as I hugged her. She tensed for a second, probably from the shock of me hugging her willingly, then she squeezed back. "I love you, you know that, right? You're a pain in my ass and kind of a bully, but I don't know what I'd do without you." I pulled back so I could look her in the eye. "You're pretty awesome, you know that right?"

She smacked my arm and got up, moving towards her room. "Of course, I know that, twat. Now I'm going to go into my room and go into a coma for a while. Don't bother me unless it's to tell me that you finally nailed Ian."

Laughing to myself I made my way into my own bedroom. It was decided. I would get some sleep, then I'd go find Ian. As difficult as it was to admit, Stacy was right. Ian was worth the risk. The problem was I didn't fear regretting taking a risk on him…I feared he would end up regretting taking the risk on me.

After sleeping for thirty-six hours straight - seriously - I headed to work. I'd taken extra time getting ready this morning. Way more than normal. I was nervous about seeing Ian. I was going to lay it all out on the line to-day. I'd told my story. I'd told it more times than I could count. But I'd never told it to someone that I was afraid of losing. Someone whose opinion mattered.

I had to talk myself out of changing my mind a hun-dred times before I got to the office. By the time the el-evators opened I could barely breathe. I was seriously afraid I might faint if I didn't manage to slow my heart rate and catch my breath.

I walked over to the kitchen to get a glass of water.

My throat was suddenly very dry and if I tried to speak right now I'd probably just choke. As I stood there sipping my ice water, a calm started to settle in. Despite my fear of rejection and of hurting Ian, I knew he cared about me. If anyone would understand and still care about me after knowing the truth, it would be him.

Excitement started to take over, washing away all my hesitation, and I started to make my way towards Ian's office. Only, before I could take more than two steps a vision of a tiny, little pest stepped into my way, blocking my path.

"Carrie," I hissed, my teeth gritted.

"Adalyn," she nodded solemnly. "I've been looking for you."

"What do you need? I'm kind of on my way to do something," I snapped, not even trying to hide my annoyance. I didn't have time for this. I needed to get to Ian before I lost all my courage.

"What I need is for you to stay away from my brother." I started to lay in to her but she got into my face. Her sudden invasion into my personal space threw me off guard enough to make me stumble backwards. "I don't know what you've done," she continued, "but Ian has been a mess. I knew you would be bad for him. I warned you to stay away from him. You are going to ruin him just like Maggie did, and he is strong enough to endure it, but it doesn't mean he should have to. You need to fix this. Whatever you did to get Ian under your spell, undo it."

"I didn't do anything, Carrie. I - " she cut me off before I could continue.

"Ian is too good. His heart is too big. He has a soft spot for the underdog. You're a broken toy to him and he can't resist trying to fix you. I've always had to look after him, making sure he didn't give too much. People always take advantage of his generosity, and it always leads to him getting hurt."

"I don't know who you think you are Carrie, but you know nothing about me. And you might not know Ian as well as you think you do, either."

She scoffed and then side stepped my retort altogether. "You have to be at least halfway decent for Stacy to care so much about you, so I've tried to give you the benefit of the doubt, but Ian has bent over backwards handing you the world on a silver platter since you walked into his life and you repaid him by hurting him. He hasn't been sleeping or eating. He's a mess, and it's because of you. I don't know what happened, but I know something did, and you need to fix it."

"Seriously, Carrie, I don't know what you're talking about. I mean yeah, Ian has helped me in a lot of ways. Looking after me, hiring me, mentoring me, and being a friend. But I haven't taken advantage of him. I mean…"

"Don't, Adalyn. Quit lying to me. There is no way

you are seriously that oblivious. All he's done since he met you was make exceptions and give you special treatment. The company phone? the sign-on bonus? No one else gets those. Even the position he hired you for didn't exist. He made one up just to give you a job. No one wanted you here, they all tried to talk him out of it. You aren't qualified and yet he still did it. You could tank his company completely but he's so infatuated with your sob story that he wouldn't even see it coming."

I wanted to be angry. I wanted to slap her. But I was too stunned. Was what she was saying true? Was everything about Ian a lie? A manipulation to get me in bed? Why would he go to such lengths for someone he didn't know? Maybe this whole time I had just been a conquest for him. Maybe he had been faking everything, playing me until he could get what he wanted.

It didn't feel right. Those thoughts didn't sound like the truth. But I couldn't help the sinking feeling that what Carrie was saying was true. Why would she lie? She may want to hurt me, but she wouldn't want to hurt Ian. If he really cared about me, then despite how she feels about me, surely she wouldn't want to destroy his relationship with me. Would she?

My mind was racing, my eyes darting back and forth as I tried to sort out what she was saying. My body started shaking and I felt like I was going to pass out or start crying any second. I needed to get out of there, clear my head.

"Look, Adalyn," Carrie said, her voice softer. "I'm not trying to be cruel. I'm not accusing you of doing anything intentionally. If you really do care about Ian at all, then you'll walk away. I don't know your story, I don't claim to know anything about you. But I know my brother and I just can't...I can't watch him go through this again."

I don't remember anything else she said. I don't remember leaving the building. I don't remember how I got home. I don't remember how long I'd been in the shower, though probably a while because the water was ice cold. But I couldn't move. I had sank down to the floor and wrapped my arms around myself as I pulled my knees to my chest. And I just cried. I cried until no tears were even coming anymore. And then I cried dry, silent sobs until I was shivering uncontrollably. I didn't know if it was from the pain or from the cold water, but it didn't matter. Nothing mattered. All the horrible things of my past didn't prepare me for this. The pain was unbearable, and for the second time in my life I wondered if I was going to make it. This time I really doubted I would.

CHAPTER 25

IAN

It was Wednesday. I hadn't seen Adalyn since Friday night when we fell asleep on the couch. It was hard not to contact her over the weekend, but knowing I would see her Monday kept me going. I wasn't going to give her as much time away from me this time. I was going to go to her and we were going to work this out.

Only she didn't come to work on Monday. I know, because I worked in her office all day so I wouldn't miss her. Finally, around 2 a.m. I headed out. It wasn't entirely unusual for employees not to come in to work one day since we didn't have set hours. So as I tossed and turned all night, I decided to get to work extra early to make sure I beat her there and wait for her in her office again.

Only she didn't show up again. By 10 p.m. Tuesday night, with no sign of Adalyn and no word from her about why she wasn't at work, I called her. It went straight to voicemail. I sent her several text messages but got no response. I debated going to her apartment but didn't know if my showing up there would only make things worse, so I tried Stacy's phone. I didn't even give Stacy time to greet me when she picked up.

"Stacy where is Adalyn? Is she okay?"

"Hello to you too, dick."

"Seriously, Stacy, she hasn't been to work and I can't get through to her. I'm worried. Is she home? Is she sick?"

"She's fine Ian, she just took a couple days off. Leave her alone."

"What? Why would you tell me to leave her alone? I'm her friend and her boss. I'm not bothering her, I'm concerned."

"Well you're bothering me. I can't talk right now. I'll call you later."

She hung up before I could say anything else. I immediately dialed her again but she must have hit ignore because after three rings it went to voicemail. What was going on? Why was everyone ignoring me? I must have been missing something.

I wanted so badly to just drive over to her apartment, demand to see her. My self control was dwindling and it was getting too hard to give her space. I had no idea what was going on with her. Why she reacted the way she had in my office, why she had cried in my arms, and then disappeared before I woke up. She was obviously avoiding me, no matter what anyone said, that was obvious. I needed to understand what I had done wrong. I needed to fix it.

Deciding I needed to calm down and compose myself before I showed up at her door and said or did something to make it worse, I headed home. My mind was on fire, not slowing long enough for me to fall asleep. But eventually my body started to shut down anyway, too worn down from my lack of sleep over the last two weeks. As I drifted off to sleep, Adalyn's face filled my thoughts. How her whole body lit up when she smiled. How her lip puffed out adorably when she was pouting. How she would chew her lip and fidget with her hands when she was nervous. And then the last thing I saw before sleep took me was the sad look in her eyes when I held her just a few days ago, and I worried it would be the last time I would ever feel her in my arms.

I must have forgotten to set my alarm because when I woke in a groggy haze it was already sunny out. I glanced at my clock and saw that it was already 9 a.m. Shit! I never slept this late. I couldn't remember the last time I'd gotten to work after 7 a.m.

I quickly showered, and needing the confidence today, I decided to wear a suit. I knew I looked good in them and the first time I'd met Adalyn I'd been wearing this very one. So much had happened since that first meeting and I had a hard time remembering what my life was like before Adalyn. Had I even really been living? Or was I still just pretending? Going through the motions of what I thought needed to be done, still hiding who I truly was.

These thoughts still plagued me as I pulled into the parking lot at work. I couldn't get upstairs fast enough. If she wasn't at work today, that was it, I was going to go look for her. Enough of these games and avoidance, it was time for me to lay it all out there and tell her how I felt and hope she could find it in herself to love me back.

I could tell she wasn't there as soon as I stepped off the elevator. The place just felt…empty. It wasn't, of course. There were people everywhere, playing games, chatting. There was loud music playing but I could barely hear it over the pounding in my ears. I just had a feeling…a horrible, sinking feeling…that today was not going to be a good day.

I was right. As I approached her office, I saw her desk first. It had been completely cleared of all personal belongings and the only thing sitting on it was her cell phone and an envelope. I knew what was in it. I didn't need to open it, but I did anyway. And my heart sank when I realized I was right about what was inside.

Dear Mr. Drake,

I am writing this letter to regretfully inform you of my resignation from Drake Designs effective immediately.
You will find I have returned the "company phone" and have also left a check for the amount of my

sign-on bonus. Taking into consideration the fact
that I did not earn this money and it is not really
"company policy" to issue sign-on bonuses to each
of it's employees, I did not feel comfortable keep-
ing it.
I wish you and your company the best of luck in
future endeavors.

Dearest Regards,
Adalyn Montgomery

Nope. She wasn't getting away that easily. I tore up the check, shoved her phone in my pocket and started toward the door. I was brought to an abrupt halt at the sight of Carrie standing in the doorway, looking guilty of something.

"What did you do, Carrie," I growled as I stalked toward her.

"I...I-I just...I was helping you, Ian!" She was pleading and tugging on my arm as I tried to pass her. "Please understand, Ian. She wasn't good for you. She was going to hurt you just like Maggie did. You've been a mess the past few weeks and I..."

"You know nothing!" I whipped around and yanked my arm free of her grasp. Carrie gasped and took a step back, looking a little fearful of how angry I was in that moment. "You don't know her, Carrie. You have no idea what you've done. What did you do to make her quit? To make her hide from me? Tell me now so I can fix it." She hesitated, looking around like she was trying to find an excuse. "NOW, Carrie! Don't lie to me. Tell me right now or this will only get worse."

"I told her the truth, okay?" She yelled, finding her courage to speak. "I told her about everything you've done for her since she started here, and how it wasn't how you normally did things. That you'd given her special treatment. That you wanted to fix her and that she was going to end up destroying you because you are too blind to see how bad she is for you."

I looked away, not able to even face my sister in that moment. Deep down I knew she thought she was helping. She thought she was doing what was best for me, but I was tired of her interfering. I had let her get away with these types of things our whole lives because of how rough everything had been for her, but now she had managed to push away the one woman I'd ever truly loved and I couldn't bear to forgive her for that right in that moment.

"It's time to grow up, Carrie. Stop trying to use my life as an excuse to avoid yours." I knew my words were harsh, but she needed to hear them. Without another word I walked out the door, leaving Carrie quietly crying behind me.

CHAPTER 26

ADALYN

Stacy had dragged me out for coffee and I was in a piss poor mood. She hadn't given me a choice though. When I had asked her to go into my office and gather my stuff, leaving behind my phone and the letter, she had agreed with the condition of coffee afterwards.

I didn't know what she was expecting. That getting me out of the apartment would make a difference in the hollowness that was currently consuming me? I was trying really hard not to be a bitch, but it was seriously difficult. I was not good company.

"I'm worried about you, Addy."

"I know."

"I'm serious."

"*I. Know.*"

"I don't know what to do for you. Tell me what to do to help you."

I sighed in resignation. I wished there was something she could do. Truth was, I had no idea what to do. I knew I was handling all of this wrong, that there were better ways to deal with loss and grief. I just wasn't ready to get over Ian. I wasn't ready to accept that it was over before it even started. I had finally given my heart to someone and he didn't even know. And probably didn't even want it.

"At least tell me what happened, Addy. Please," she begged, reaching for my hand, but not looking surprise when I pulled away before she could touch me.

"It doesn't matter, Stace. There is no point in reliving it, it will only make you angry. Angry at people who are important in your life and I don't want to be the reason you have trouble with them. All that matters right now is that I need to find a new job."

The waitress walked over with our drinks right then, and as she handed me my coffee she smiled sweetly down at me. "Did you say you're looking for a job?"

"Oh, um, yes. I am."

"We're hiring right now, need someone to start immediately. If you're interested, I could introduce you to the owner real quick."

"Oh, actually that would be great. Thank you."

Working at a coffee shop? Not exactly a step in the right direction, but it was a job. It would be a distraction. It didn't matter anymore what I did with my time and whether or not I enjoyed it. All the fight left in me was gone. Being stubborn and demanding required too much energy. It required you to care, and I didn't care. Not about anything. Not anymore.

Two hours later I was already starting my first shift. Stacy had left shortly after I met with the manager, leaving to run errands and after making me promise over and over that I was okay. I wasn't, but I needed a job and I couldn't stand another day of sitting around the apartment crying incessantly. So I lied, told her I was fine, and just hoped that eventually that would end up being true.

CHAPTER 27

IAN

"Adalyn."

She turned to face me with a look of shock and anger, though I had a feeling it wasn't directed at me after hearing her mumble Stacy's name under her breath.

"Don't be mad at Stacy. I had to practically threaten her life to get her to tell me where you were. How did you get a job already? It's only been a day."

"They needed someone to start immediately and I had nothing else to do and I can't afford to be out of work. At least not without people making 'exceptions' for me."

Ignoring that jab and the glare she was giving me, I gently pulled on her elbow, pleading with my eyes. "Please, Adalyn, can we talk? I didn't sleep all night and I panicked when you weren't at work this morning. I've been all over the city looking for you. I just need a few minutes to explain."

"You had plenty of time to explain last night, Ian but you didn't say anything. And I can't just walk out of here, I literally just started. I don't think they would appreciate me taking a break an hour into my shift."

"I know, I'm sorry, just please. Give me five minutes."

She sighed but took my arm, leading me through the back of the coffee shop and out the back door, out into an alley behind the building. The rain had turned into a downpour and even under the awning, we were getting wet.

"Hurry up, Ian, I have to get back," she said, crossing her arms. The impatient and tense stance of her body caused my confidence to falter slightly, but now was no time to back down.

"Adalyn, listen. I know we haven't known each other all that long. It doesn't take a genius to see that there is more going on with you than you let on. If you would just tell me...just open up to me...trust me...I wouldn't blur the lines. I wasn't trying to hurt you, I just wanted to help you."

"That's the problem, Ian. You treat me like a charity case. Like I'm in need of saving, but I'm not. Yeah, things may get worse before they get better but I can take care of myself. I never asked for or wanted special treatment. Do you know how humiliated I am? Even if I was willing to look past all of this, I can't step foot in that place ever again."

"Adalyn, please, I'm sorry Carrie was a bitch. She should never have talked to you like that. It will never happen again. Maybe you're right, maybe I was trying to save you. But it wasn't because I thought you were helpless or because I wanted to control you, I just wanted...I don't know... I wanted to make a difference in your life. I wanted you to look at me and be happy. You hated me so much at first. Nothing I was saying or doing was helping. I didn't know what else to do. I just wanted to matter to you."

"Why, Ian? Why!" She was yelling now. I could feel the old Ian seeping back in and I wanted to cower as she approached me, but I couldn't. This was too important. She was too important. Now was the time to be a man.

"You don't know me. I haven't even been nice to you. Yeah, we've shared a few good times, but for the most part I've been horrible. I'm no better than your ex, so why would you want anything to do with me? Do you just like being treated horribly? I don't like who I am around you. I turn into this horrible, bitchy person because of how you make me feel, and I can't do it any more. I don't want to do it any more," she said, dropping her arms to her sides and letting out a long breath, her shoulders drooping as if a weight had been lifted all of a sudden.

"What do you feel, Adalyn? What do I make you feel?" She turned her back to me and walked right out into the rain. "Where are you going?" I yelled, chasing after her.

"I'm leaving. I'm walking away from another job because of you. Because I can't possibly go back in there right now looking like this. I just need to go home."

"Let me drive you," I pleaded, grabbing her elbow, urging her to turn and face me.

Tears were streaming down her face, mixing with the rain. Her hair was flat against her cheeks, her clothes completely soaked through. She looked broken and defeated. I had made her feel that way. Knowing her pain was my fault felt like a sucker punch to my gut. Reaching up in a gesture of wiping her tears off of her face, despite the rain having already done so, she leaned into my hand.

As if realizing what she had just done, she pulled her face away from my hand and stepped back. "I can't do this, Ian. I'm no good for you. You deserve better than me. I'm too messed up, I'm too far gone." I tried to reach for her but she took another step back. "No, Ian, don't. I don't need you to fix me. I've accepted who I am and I'm okay with it, but that doesn't mean I'm okay with dragging you into my mess. I care...I just...it wouldn't be fair to you."

Closing the gap between us in one swift move, I grabbed her hands before she could move away from me again. Gently lifting her chin with my hand, I looked her in the eyes and tried to show her everything I was feeling. Desperate for her to see me, to see that I truly meant everything I was saying.

"You aren't too far gone, Adalyn. You're right here.

I'm here. Letting someone help you isn't the same as being weak. Leaning on someone for strength doesn't make you helpless. I don't want to control you, I don't want to fix you. I just want to be a part of you, any way you'll let me. I want to be there when you need to cry, or yell or laugh. I don't want to make you do anything, I just want to be there to experience it with you. Just let me be a part of your life, Adalyn. Please."

For a split second her face completely relaxed and her body sagged into mine, but a look of sadness overtook whatever emotion she was fighting off and she started to pull away again.

"Ian, you are amazing. I would be incredibly lucky to have you in my life, but I care about you too much to let you in. I can't let you in. You deserve someone uncomplicated, who will treat you how you deserve. I don't want to be another regret in your life."

"You aren't her, Adalyn. You pushing me away out of fear of getting hurt isn't the same as being mean just for the sake of hurting me. You are nothing like her, so don't for a second think I would ever compare you to her. I never felt for her what I feel for you, not even for a minute. I was trapped and weak, but I'm not that person any more. I don't feel an obligation to you, Adalyn, I just want you. Let me in," I begged, looking her square in the eyes. "Let me love you."

The shock of what I'd just said resonated throughout her whole body. Her knees gave out and she started to collapse. She was shivering and we were still standing in the rain. Grabbing her waist, I lifted her up and took her hand, wrapping it around my waist. We started toward my car, neither of us speaking. I knew she was processing. I hadn't meant to say it, but I didn't regret it either. I would have said it much sooner if I knew it wouldn't scare her away. But I wasn't going anywhere anymore. She could run, she could push me away, but she would never get rid of me. It was time for her to accept that and to realize that she could count on me.

I opened the door and started to help her into the passenger seat of my car. She seemed almost catatonic. I was desperate for her to say something, anything, give me some kind of idea what was going on in her head. I didn't expect her to say it back, we still had a lot to work through and I imagined it would be a while before she would trust me enough to allow herself to return my feelings. But the thought of her feeling nothing, of her not wanting me and not wanting to even try...I couldn't bear it. It would tear me apart, but no matter what she said, I was staying. If all I could be in her life was a friend then I would take it.

She removed her arm from around my waist and started to get in, but froze when she leaned down. "Adalyn," I whispered, reaching my hand out to see if she needed help. She grabbed my hand and whipped herself around to face me, and before I could ask what she was doing, her mouth was on mine. It was a hungry, desperate kiss. I could feel her pouring every fear, every hesitation into the kiss, and I happily took all those emotions from her. I wanted to bear their burden as my own. I wanted to take some of the weight off of her, help her carry around whatever pain it was she was harboring.

Our hands were everywhere, exploring every inch of each other over our soaking wet clothes. We were undoubtedly making a spectacle of ourselves out on the sidewalk, groping each other like teenagers, but I couldn't have cared less. Adalyn was finally in my arms and I wasn't going to let anything ruin this moment. If it was the only one she ever gave me, then I need to make the most of every second she was mine.

Adalyn pulled away and I groaned in response, the loss of contact pulling me out of our kiss induced haze.

"Let's go," she whispered, leaning into my ear.

She wasn't running. At least not from me, but with me. She wasn't shutting down or lashing out, instead, she was looking at me with what I wanted so badly to believe was love in her eyes. Not wanting to waste another minute, worried she would shut down again any second, I hurried her into the car and ran around to the driver's side. I only lived fifteen minutes away, but after running every stop light and breaking every traffic law known to man, I made a new record and we made it to my place in eight minutes.

She had been holding my hand the entire way home, softly rubbing circles on my palm with her thumb. I hesitated, almost afraid to look at her, fearing she would have changed her mind already. She didn't look angry or closed off, though, she looked...scared. That twinkle from a few minutes ago when we kissed was still there, but she was chewing her bottom lip and having trouble making eye contact.

"We need to talk, Ian."

CHAPTER 28

ADALYN

I couldn't believe I was about to do this. I had told plenty of people what Ian thinks is my 'secret,' but never to someone whose opinion mattered. I'd had my heart closed off for so long that the thought of opening it up and allowing someone to hurt me was more than terrifying. The last time I had made the decision to tell Ian I had ended up walking away with my heart in pieces. I knew it was different this time, though, and I needed to face whatever was going to happen next.

He said he loved me, but that could change. What I was about to tell him could change things forever, but he deserved the truth. He deserved to know who it was he thought he was in love with so he could figure out if that's truly how he felt.

And I deserved it. I deserved love, and the only way I'd be able to believe him is if he knew everything. So taking a deep breath, I shifted in the passenger seat to face Ian. Eye contact was required for this conversation. I needed him to see in my eyes that I was not weak.

"Before I tell you this, my 'secret,' I need you to promise me that you will tell me the truth afterward. You said you love me, but you can't love me." I held up my hand to keep him from speaking. I needed to just get this

out. "I'm not saying ever, but you can't truly love someone if you don't really know who they are. I need you to
know, though, I am not broken. I don't need to be fixed.
If you don't feel the same way after this, you have my
word that I will not hold it against you. No one would
understand better than me. So you have to promise to be
honest with me."

Pausing to wait for his answer, he pressed his lips
into a flat line, his jaw clenched and he nodded.

"I was raped in college." He immediately tensed up
and his chest started heaving. I placed my hand on his to
calm him down, giving him a minute to slow his heart
rate. I needed him to really hear everything that came
next.

"I have no delusions as to what kind of damage that
has caused in me. I have issues from it, I'm still working
them out, but let me tell you again. I. Am. Not. Broken.
What happened to me was horrible and I'd give anything
to go back and be able to prevent it from happening, but
I can't change the past, so I've found ways to cope moving forward."

Looking away for a brief second, I tried to gain my
composure, but when I turned back to face him the look
on his face had changed.

"Stop it," I said, pointing my finger in his face.
"That look, right there, stop that. It's instinct, human nature, and I get that look every time I tell my story. It's

pity and sadness. I don't need you to mourn for me, Ian. I don't need someone to feel sorry for me. I can handle that look from strangers, but not from you." He started to speak up again, but I interrupted him. "You don't have to defend yourself. I'm not saying that's how you feel. I've made enough assumptions and snap judgments about you already, I'm not going to keep doing that. But I need to make sure you really understand what I'm telling you, and the only way to do that is to show you."

"Show me?"

"I'm going to take you to the place I go to every Friday afternoon. We can finish this discussion after that. There's more, Ian. If you really want to know me, then you have to really know me. All of me. You can't pick and choose which parts - you take the good with the bad."

"Where to?" he asked, turning the engine and backing out of the driveway.

Twenty minutes later we were pulling up to an old building on the outskirts of downtown. From the outside it looked run down, but it had become a second home to me. Neither of us had said a word on the way here, though I could see Ian fighting the urge to say something by biting his cheek. The rain had stopped and the sun had come out. It was actually turning into a beautiful day.

"What is this place?"

"You'll see," I said, putting my hand in Ian's and pulling him in behind me.

"Addy!" Three girls ran up and bear hugged me, giant grins on their faces.

"Hey, sweeties! How you doing today?"

"We're okay," the youngest one, Sara, spoke up. She was only 10 years old. "Lora is having a rough day though. We've done everything we can to cheer her up but nothing is working."

Giving Sara a quick squeeze, I told Ian I would be right back and walked over to Lora. I spent a few minutes talking to her, but she was in no mood to talk. Heading back over to Ian, I found him leaning against a wall, staring at me intently.

"Penny for your thoughts?"

"Just wondering what we're doing here. You ever going to tell me what this place is?"

"It's a rape crisis center. I volunteer here on the weekends, on Fridays is when I have my counseling sessions. I both give and receive counseling."

Just then the director, Marti, walked over and hugged me. "Are you going to introduce me to your handsome friend, Addy?" she asked with a wink in Ian's direction. He actually blushed! Where is a camera when you need one.

"Marti, this is Ian, a friend of mine. Ian, this is Marty. She is the director here and the person who so kindly welcomed me and took a chance on a stranger."

"Oh, hush Adalyn. We are blessed to have you. After the work you did back at UV, we would have been fools to pass up an opportunity to have you here helping us." Turning to look at Ian, she continued to embarrass me. "Adalyn is beloved by all the girls. She has already impacted so many of their lives. Some of these girls have been coming here for years and no one has been able to make an impact, but Addy here has a unique way of getting through to them. I've never seen anything like it. She is quite amazing."

"That she is," Ian said, turning to look at me affectionately. It was my turn to blush then.

"Well, Marti, we just wanted to stop in and say hello. We won't take up any more of your time. I'll see you on Friday."

"It was lovely to meet you, Marti," Ian said, taking her hand and placing a chaste kiss on the top. Now Marty was blushing, but she quickly turned to me and gave me a hug, seeing us off as we left.

"Want to take a walk?"

"Only if you'll hold my hand. I just...I just need..." I ended his torture by slipping my hand in his.

"I'd love nothing more."

We walked in silence for a couple blocks until we reached a small park. Making our way over to a bench that overlooked a small pond, still holding hands, I was feeling braver by the second. He hadn't ran yet. He wasn't avoiding me. Most men had a tendency to go one of two ways when they found out something like this about a woman.

There were the men who suddenly treated you as if you would break. Like now that they knew the truth all of a sudden you were made of porcelain and even being near you would cause you to shatter into a million pieces.

Then there were the men who looked at you with disgust. Honestly, in my experience it was a visceral re-action, it almost couldn't be helped. Some men didn't like to share, and the thought of their woman having been violated made her suddenly repulsive in their eyes. Didn't make it okay to feel that way, but the majority of people just didn't know how to react.

None of this had ever happened to me, I'd just watched it happen to other girls at the shelters, the one back home and the one here. I'd never allowed myself to care enough about a man for that conversation to be necessary.

"So do you think you're ready?" I asked Ian, bend-ing at the waist to catch his eye as he looked at the ground. He sat back against the bench and squeezed my hand tighter, a sign for me to go ahead.

"It happened my freshman year. Before I tell you what happened, I want you to know that I was broken for a while. I went through phases. First, I didn't want anyone to touch me. Not even my parents. I was practically agoraphobic. The only person I would even let near me was Stacy, because she never tried to talk. We would just sit in complete silence, next to each other on my bed, for hours at a time. I'll never be able to repay her for that, her giving up so much of her time to just sit with me."

"There was a trial. Having to prepare for that brought me out of my shell. I was angry. So angry. I wanted them to pay. I went to counseling, worked with the lawyers, and when the time came I was ready. I wasn't scared anymore, I wasn't hiding. I refused to let them win any longer."

What came next was the hardest part for me. Even harder than describing the rape itself.

"After the trial is when I really went off the deep end. I just couldn't hold it in anymore. They were all found not guilty, my rapists just set free into the world, as if what happened to me didn't even matter. Not even a slap on the wrist. I never found out how they managed that. We had plenty of evidence, even eye witnesses. I heard sometime later that someone had paid off the judge, but who knows if that's true."

"Anyway, I was desperate to get some control back in my life. Nothing made me feel more helpless than when that verdict came back. It was worse than being raped. People who were supposed to protect me were letting my rapists go. I was so angry. I just snapped. I can't even tell you how many guys I slept with. I wish I could tell you I was drunk or high and that something was causing me to not think rationally, but I was always sober. I won't tell you the things I did during that time. I mean, I would if you really wanted to know them, but I don't think you would."

"I continued going to therapy, only because the college required it in order for me to be able to take a lighter class load without losing my scholarship. I felt like I was coping, but I really wasn't, it was a charade. I was just in denial. Stacy is the only thing that kept me grounded. She never judged me, never lectured me. She was just there, supporting me, and she went with me to the crisis center on campus on a day that I was feeling particularly depressed. Thanks to the counselors and other survivors there, I came back to reality and stopped my self destructive behavior. That was 3 years ago. I haven't had sex since."

His jaw dropped, but he quickly tried to recover. I couldn't help but giggle at his reaction. He was trying hard not to show any emotion, and I fell for him a little more for it.

"Adalyn," he whispered, softly squeezing my hand. "You said 'them.' How many...I mean, what...only if you want to tell me...I just…"

"It's fine, Ian. I want to tell you." I took a deep breath and paused for a moment. "I've told this story hundreds of times. The crisis center helped me so much, I wanted to give back. I've traveled a lot, going to campuses to speak to the girls, trying to help prevent for them what I couldn't prevent for myself. It's important to me that you know, I am not afraid. I'm not afraid to talk about this, and I am not ashamed. It's not a secret, it's just a part of who I am now. The reason I didn't tell you sooner...."

I turned to look him in the eye. "I've never told anyone I cared about. I haven't been in a relationship. Not because I'm afraid, but because I didn't want to. I wasn't ready. I had to make myself whole again before I could open up to someone else. I knew I had to be the one to fix me, I couldn't depend on someone else to do it for me. Honestly, it never even really occurred to me to want to tell someone. No one had affected me the way you did, and the loss of control over my emotions made me act out. I'm sorry for how I treated you."

"You have nothing to be sorry for, Adalyn. There's nothing you could have said or done to scare me away. I knew the minute I looked at you that I was meant to know you. You're not the only one who can be stubborn," he said, giving me a cocky smile. "And nothing you say or do now will change it either. I'm ready, Adalyn. Tell me, trust me. Let me prove to you that I'm not going anywhere."

"It was freshman year. I had been dating this guy, your typical cocky college jock. He was a senior and gorgeous and I couldn't believe it when he asked me out. I knew his reputation, but he was only ever really sweet to me. Eventually I caved and let him take me on a date. He was charming and easy to talk to, and we started spending more and more time together. I wasn't a virgin, I had slept with my high school boyfriend, but I wasn't in a hurry to take that leap with anyone else yet either."

"One night at his place, we were laying on his bed watching a movie, something we'd done several times already. We were kissing, doing some heavy petting, nothing too crazy. When he started to slip his hand under the hem of my shirt, I stopped him. He looked frustrated at first, but we went back to kissing. When he tried it again, I got frustrated. He started yelling at me, calling me a tease. Saying how he'd never worked this hard for a girl before and how I should feel lucky he was even spending time with me."

"He was like a different person. I'd never seen him act like that. I grabbed my bag and ran out. He lived in a frat house so there were at least a dozen guys in the living room as I headed for the door, but before I could reach the door handle, he grabbed me and shoved me back around to face him. I smacked him across his face and called him an asshole and took off running. I could hear the other frat guys yelling and laughing and giving him a hard time, but he stood on the front porch screaming at me. I don't even know what he was saying, I was running so fast I couldn't hear anything."

I loosened my grip on Ian's hand and he flexed his fingers. I didn't realize how hard I had been squeezing it.

"He left me alone after that. I expected him to give me a hard time around campus or spread rumors about me, but life pretty much went back to normal. If I saw him around he would just avoid me, no one ever bothered me. I even let myself wonder if I had been wrong about him. That thought didn't last long, though."

"There was a party at his frat house one night. Stacy begged me to go and even though I still didn't want to see him, I was curious to find out if I really had been wrong about him, so I agreed to go. By the time we got there the party was going full force. We weren't two steps in the door before red solo cups were shoved in our hands, full of warm beer. I had never really drank before. It was never worth the risk of getting in trouble when I was working so hard for scholarships. But I was nervous and figured it wouldn't kill me to just act my age for once, and before I knew it, I had drank it all."

"It didn't take long for the room to start spinning and for the people to become blurry. I figured the alcohol would affect me more than others since I never drank, but I could tell something wasn't right. I couldn't see anyone's faces clearly enough to be able to find Stacy, so I just walked around yelling for her. Someone grabbed my arm and said he knew where Stacy was and would take me to her. I had no choice but to trust him, I could barely walk at this point."

Ian's entire body tensed up at that moment, and I knew he was preparing for what I was about to say.

"He led me up some stairs and into a bedroom. I could tell by the voices talking that there were several other people in the room, but they were all just blurry figures by this point. I asked where Stacy was, and one of them laughed and mumbled something I couldn't hear. The next thing I knew, I was laying on the bed and I could feel my clothes being pulled off of me, but I was too weak to resist. I was trying to yell but I honestly couldn't tell if any sound was even coming out."

"It felt like I had been in there for hours. I couldn't make out their faces, but I could make out the shapes of five guys. Three of them had their turn with me before the door flew open. I turned my head toward the light coming from the hallway and heard Stacy yell for some-one, then she ran over to me and covered me up with a blanket. Suddenly I was wrapped in someone's arms, being carried down the stairs. I could hear whispers and shrieking cries, but it wasn't until we were outside that I realized I was the one crying."

"The last thing I remember was screaming and clutching to the man holding me, begging them not to take me in the ambulance. I didn't even know who was holding me, but I felt safe and I was terrified to be alone.

Eventually I was ripped from his arms and put into an ambulance, sobbing. Whatever medicine they gave me on the way to the hospital knocked me out and I don't remember anything else that happened over the next two days."

I paused, giving Ian a chance to let it all sink in. I expected him to avoid eye contact, to subtly move away from me, but he surprised me by taking my hands in his and turning to face me. I couldn't even tell you what he was feeling at that moment. It wasn't the pity and disgust I was expecting. It was...understanding? How could he understand when it had never happened to him?

"I was there, Adalyn."

"You were where?"

"The man who carried you...that was me."

"What? How is that...I mean...how is that possible? Why didn't you ever say something?"

"I didn't realize it was you until just now. Your hair was different and your face was buried in my neck, I never really got a look at your face. I asked Stacy about you later but she wouldn't talk about it. I never even knew your name."

"What were you doing there? You didn't go to school there," I shook my head, trying to process this new information. I still couldn't believe what he was telling me.

"I was visiting a friend and Stacy begged me to meet

her there to say hi. I...I tried to go with you. I begged
them to let me ride in the ambulance, to not force you
out of my arms. You were so terrified and I felt this fierce
protectiveness over you. When they finally tore you out
of my arms, the cops had to restrain me. I was screaming
and clawing, trying to get to you. I followed the ambulance to the hospital but they wouldn't let me see you
because I wasn't family. I sat in the waiting room for two
full days before Stacy made me go home. No one would
tell me anything, only that you were recovering. I was so
frustrated. I asked Stacy over and over for years to tell
me who you were and what happened but she wouldn't.
It caused us to not speak for an entire year, actually."

"I just...I can't believe this. I...I knew there had to
be a reason," I said in disbelief. Then to both our surprise, I smiled.

"What did you know Adalyn? Why are you smiling
like that?" He looked confused but he was smiling back
and all I wanted in that moment was to throw myself into
his arms.

"I just knew. Or, at least my body did. You are the
only person since that night that I've felt comfortable
around. The only one I didn't cringe and move away
from when I was touched. Every time you were near me
I felt...calm. It scared the shit out of me. It's part of why
I pushed you away so much. Pretty messed up, right? I
pushed you away because I felt comfortable around you.

It sounds crazy, but I just hadn't felt like that in so long it was foreign to me. Somehow, I just...knew."

Ian cupped my face in his hands and brushed his thumb across my lower lip. "Thank you, Adalyn. Thank you for trusting me, for opening up to me. You're amazing. I don't pity you, I don't think you're broken. I think you're strong and brave and just...amazing. Telling me all of that...it doesn't change how I feel. It only confirms what I already knew. I love you, Adalyn. I love you."

The sincerity in his voice and the love in his eyes stole my breath, and for a moment I couldn't speak. Searching his eyes for something, anything, to tell me what was happening wasn't real, I felt the last of my defenses melt away when all I saw looking back at me was admiration.

"I love you too, Ian. I love you so much." The next thing I knew Ian had scooped me up, holding me the same way he had that night, and he carried me all the way back to his car, with my face buried in his neck.

CHAPTER 29

IAN

When we arrived back at my apartment, I helped Adalyn out of my car and led her up to the door by the hand, careful not to rush even though I was dying to have her in my bed. To show her just how much I meant it when I said I loved her.

Adalyn clung to my arm, her head resting on my shoulder, her hand stroking up and down my arm in a loving gesture. The sexual tension between us was thick, but the calmness from our declarations of love and having everything finally out in the open relaxed us both enough to make the trip to my apartment door bearable.

After I locked the door behind us, Adalyn took my hand and led us both towards my bedroom. I was happy to let Adalyn set the pace of what was about to happen. She deserved my patience and understanding, and any desire I had to tear her clothes off of her and throw her onto my bed was easily pushed aside. I loved her, I would give her everything. If control was what she needed, she could have it.

We stood there, just looking at each other, for several seconds. I wanted to give Adalyn the chance to speak first, make the first move, letting her know I was handing over the control. Just when I thought the sexual tension might break me, she took a step forward.

"I want to give you the control, Ian," she said as she pressed her hands to my chest and looked into my eyes. I stared hard into her eyes, wanting to make sure she really meant what she was saying and wasn't just trying to give me what she thought I needed.

"I mean it, Ian. I trust you. I want this…I want to give myself to you entirely. I've never done that before, and the thought of doing that in the past would have been too much. But I'm not scared, Ian. Not even a little. I love you and I want to give you everything, all of me." She spoke with love in her voice and pleading in her eyes, and I fell in love with her even more in that moment. This woman before me had endured the unspeakable and she had every right to feel the need to have control, yet she was giving it to me. A gift. A gift I would never take for granted.

I slowly pulled her shirt over her head, never breaking eye contact. Next, I undid the button of her jeans and slowly slid them down her thighs, still staring at her, watching for any uncertainty that would tell me we were going too fast. I took a moment to appreciate Adalyn standing in my bedroom in only a pink lacy bra and matching thong. She was the epitome of perfection.

I slipped one hand around her waist and deftly unclasped her bra, watching it slide slowly down her arms and onto the floor. I couldn't wait any long, so I reached out and caressed her breasts, appreciating the softness of her skin, my cock straining against my zipper as she dropped her head back and let out a small moan.

I took her hand and led her over to the bed and motioned for her to climb in. She sat in the middle of the bed, watching as I removed all of my clothes in the same painstakingly slow process as hers. I had been dreaming of having Adalyn in my bed for months, and even my wildest fantasies never came close to the beauty of her laying on my bed, her eyes dark with lust as she licked her lips slowly.

I climbed onto the bed and hovered over her, raising myself with my forearms and continued to stare into her eyes for several more minutes. I wanted to savor this moment, this night, engrain the memory of how she looked and felt the first time she gave herself to me.

I reached over to one of the bed side tables and opened the drawer, grabbing a condom, but Adalyn placed her hand gently on mine and shook her head. I trusted her completely, and without needing any further assurances, I sat up on my knees and pulled her thong down her legs then tossed it across the room.

"You are so beautiful," I whispered before giving her a gentle kiss.

"I love you, Ian," she choked out as I entered her, finally knowing what it felt like to be whole. Adalyn was my present, my future, my everything. As I continued to slowly move in and out of her, feeling her climax approaching, I brushed her hair off of her face and kissed her like it was my last day on earth.

"I love you too, Adalyn."

I wasn't sure how long we had been holed up in my apartment. We'd turned our phones off hours ago and the sun had risen and set at least twice. We spent the entire time naked, ordering in take out, watching movies and generally enjoying our time together. Oh yeah, and having lots of sex.

"You should probably turn your phone on. I'm sure people are going crazy trying to reach you, seeing as how you own a business and all," Adalyn said as she traced the contours of my stomach lightly with her finger.

"If it's an emergency they know where I live. It's taken me months to get you naked, and I'm going to keep you that way for as long as I can," I replied as I kissed her hair and pulled her tighter to my side.

"Well I should probably at least call Stacy. She's probably freaking out."

"I sent her and my work an email saying we were together and not to bother us after you fell asleep a few nights ago. I wasn't going to risk having someone come barging in here, interrupting my naked time with you."

Adalyn playfully pinched my side and hopped out

of bed before I could retaliate. "What was that for?"

"For holding me hostage, apparently. I thought I was a willing participant but I'm starting to think this was all orchestrated," she teased and she backed herself up towards the door.

I climbed off the bed and started slowly stalking towards her. "Where do you think you're going, Sunshine? I'm not done with you yet."

Then she bolted, running out of the door and down the hallway. I caught up to her when she reached the living room and she stood behind the far end of the couch, using it as a shield between us.

"I know you're not actually trying to escape, Adalyn."

"How do you know?" Realization dawned on her and she looked down to see she was still naked. I had to admit I was enjoying this game of naked cat and mouse, getting to watch her body bounce in all the right places and she jumped behind different objects in the room to keep distance between us.

"Get over here, Adalyn," I ordered calmly. When she shook her head, I pounced. She narrowly dodged my attack, but I managed to wrap an arm around her waist, pulling her toward me. We fell back onto the couch, Adalyn on top of me, panting and laughing. Her eyes went dark when she felt my growing arousal against her thigh.

"You are insatiable, Mr. Drake," Adalyn whispered

breathlessly.

"Only when it comes to you, Sunshine. I will never get enough," I replied softly as I brushed her hair behind her ear so I could look into her eyes. I pulled her into a deep kiss and we spent hours tangled up in each other, too content to bother moving from the couch.

Damn, I loved this woman.

CHAPTER 30

ADALYN

After eleven straight days of being naked with Ian, I begrudgingly joined the human populace and started wearing clothes again.

It felt awkward going in to work knowing what I did about the special treatment Ian had given me. He assured me over and over that the only person who cared was Carrie, and that most employees had no idea of anything he had done for me. I loved my job, though, and I was happy to be back. I would just have to deal with any awkward hurdles as they arose.

Awkward hurdle number one? Carrie. And that one I wasn't going to wait for. That one needed to happen right away. If I was going to have any kind of future with Ian, I needed his sister to not be such a raving bitch. I knew they were close and so like it or not, Carrie and I were going to find a way to make amends.

She was working in one of our studios, working on the choreography to one of the video games we'd been commissioned, and I stood back watching her for a few minutes before I approached. She really was a very graceful dancer, and watching her in her element like this she looked much happier than all the other times I'd seen her. Maybe I was being too hard on her. If anyone should be willing to give second chances, it should be me.

Right as I resolved to offer an olive branch, she spotted me and she immediately looked angry but that quickly turned to something akin to…guilt? If she actually felt bad for her behavior then this talk would definitely go over a lot smoother.

"Hi Adalyn," she whispered as she approached me, never once making eye contact.

"Carrie," I replied curtly.

"I'm actually glad you're here. If you have a minute…I mean would you mind to…" she sighed frustratedly. "Can we talk?" she finally huffed out.

I couldn't help but laugh. We were so uncomfortable and horrible at this. I thought she would get mad at my laughing, but she surprised me by joining in.

"I'm sorry, I suck at this. I just want to apologize. Do you have a minute?" Her eyes looked genuine and I was glad to know this was going to be easier than I thought. Maybe Carrie and I stood a chance of actually becoming friends.

I followed her over to a couple of folded chairs that were set off to the side and accepted the bottle of water she offered me, thankful to have something to do with my hands other than fidget.

"I'm sorry," we both started at the same time, sending us both into a fit of laughter again. "You first," I said, taking a drink of my water.

"I'm sorry for how I've treated you, Adalyn. I'm not sure how much of my history Stacy or my brother has told you, but it's still no excuse for how I've behaved. I'm just basically a toddler, I have a hard time sharing. I felt threatened by you with Stacy, I was afraid I'd lose my best friend, when I should have been trying to get to know you. I was hoping maybe you could give me another chance. That maybe I could make it up to you somehow. I see how much my brother cares about you and if the two most important people in my life both care about you so much, then you must obviously be worth it. I just hope one day you can forgive me."

All my anger and resentment towards Carrie in that moment dissipated. She looked small and afraid and I couldn't find it in me to still hate her.

"I've already forgiven you, Carrie," I smiled as she looked up in surprise. "I understand what you've been going through. I can't say that it's necessarily okay how you acted towards me, but I get it. No, Ian didn't tell me much about your past, he said it was your story to tell and I hope that one day you and I can become close enough that you will feel comfortable enough with me to open up about it."

I reached out and took her hand in mine. The gesture probably surprised me more than it did her, but I loved Ian, and I wanted to be a part of his life in every way. That included his family, and she looked so vulnerable that I couldn't help but want to reach out and comfort her.

"I love your brother. I don't have to tell you how amazing he is. And you were probably right when you said, I probably don't deserve him."

"Adalyn, I was way out of line saying…"

"No, it's okay," I said, interrupting her. "It's the truth. And honestly, there might not be a woman on this earth who actually does deserve someone like Ian. And for some crazy reason, I am lucky enough to be the one who he chose to love. I won't ever take that for granted. I want you to know that I will always cherish his love, and I will spend my life trying to be the person he deserves."

I wiped away a rogue tear that escaped and gave an embarrassed smile at my show of emotion.

"I'm not usually emotional like this, but I guess love will do that to you," I laughed weakly. "I want us to be close, Carrie. I was hoping you would want that to."

"I would really, really love that Adalyn," Carrie said as she jumped up and down in her seat excitedly. She looked so youthful that it was almost hard to believe she was the same age as me.

"Okay great, because I need your help with something"

Carrie and I spent the rest of the day working on the

upcoming fundraiser our company was sponsoring. We only had two weeks to make all the changes necessary and it was probably going to require almost all of our free time just to make our plan happen. We had to contact all the vendors and planning coordinators involved and had to swear everyone to secrecy.

Convincing Carrie to help me hadn't been nearly as difficult as I thought it was going to be. Then again, our entire relationship had taken a complete turn in the days that followed our heart to heart as well. Once we hashed out all of our concerns and cleared the air, the conversation came easy between us. And the more time we spent together the more she grew on me. I truly liked Carrie and found myself regretting having not taken the time to do this with her sooner.

Keeping Ian from finding out what we were doing had been tricky, but my blossoming friendship with Carrie was a good cover. As the fundraiser neared, I became increasingly nervous. I kept waiting for a hitch in the plan, a snag in the code, for someone to accidentally spill the secret to Ian. But that wasn't the only thing I had to worry about. Not only was I worried about us actually being able to pull off our plan, but I would be in the same vicinity as Maggie. From what Carrie had told me, there was almost definitely an altercation in my near future.

Not that I wouldn't love the chance to bitch slap her, but this fundraiser was going to be a special night for Ian.

At least, I hoped it would. So as much as I would really, really love to put Maggie in her place, I would have to be the bigger person.

A couple days before the event Carrie and I went to pick up Stacy and take her shopping to get dresses for the event. We still hadn't told Stacy what was going on. She was seriously the worst secret keeper. Ever. Don't tell Stacy anything you don't want repeated. But time was running out and she would need a dress so we had no choice.

I'd been staying with Ian since the day I told him everything and had been spending so much time with Carrie with all the planning that I hadn't really had a chance to see Stacy very much, and seeing her running down the stairs from her apartment towards the car threw a pang of guilt into me. Then she opened her mouth and all that guilt dissipated.

"Move, bitch. You don't get to disappear for weeks and then get to sit shotgun. Back seat, baby."

Groaning, I got out of the passenger side of Carrie's car and moved to the back.

"Alright, so you sluts need to tell me where we're going on this mystery girls day out that I called off work for. Not that I mind playing hooky, but I'd like to know what I'm doing today that's such a secret you couldn't tell me over the phone."

Carrie looked at me in the rearview mirror and we

exchanged a knowing glance.

"Okay, seriously. I'm glad you guys made up and are in love now and all, but I don't like feeling left out. Someone better start talking or I'm going to start throwing some high fives to your faces."

We spent the drive filling Stacy in on our plans. By the time we finally finished, she was already cussing us out.

"I can't believe it. I can't believe you guys. You're such bitches. Why would you leave me out? I could have helped! Were you just afraid that all my ideas would have been better than yours? Whatever. I'm not talking to either of you all day. And every dress you try on I'm going to tell you makes you look fat," she huffed as she pouted and crossed her arms over her chest.

Carrie and I planked her on either side of her and wrapped her up into a big group hug.

"What happened to you, Adalyn? Keeping secrets from me and now hugging? It's like I don't know you anymore. It's freaking weird."

"Oh, come on," I said, linking our arms and guiding us into the boutique where we were going to be trying on dresses. "I'm still me, just an improved version. It's just been too long since we hung out. Let's fix that today and try to enjoy ourselves getting prettied up. My treat."

That got her. "Fine, if you're paying then I'll forgive you."

I'd really missed my friend.

"I am really dreading this fundraiser tonight."

"Don't be that way, Ian," I said as I straightened his tie. He was devilishly handsome in his black designer suit. As handsome as he was in a suit though, I preferred Ian in his goofy t-shirts and glasses. "It will be fine. I can handle myself. Maggie isn't going to cause any issues and this is an important event for the company."

"I know," he sighed, wrapping his arms around my waist. "I just don't know why she's coming tonight. The last time she was at this event was the night she cheated on me. And while in retrospect it turned out to be one of the best nights of my life because it finally opened my eyes to how horrible she was, I still have no desire to see her. If she so much as looks at you funny, I might not be able to control my actions."

I yanked on his tie and pulled his mouth to mine in a quick, rough kiss. "I know you're tough, Kent, but I can handle myself. I'm pretty bad ass, too, so if she knows what's good for her, she'll stay far away. Trust me, I'm not worried, okay? Let's just try to have a good time. It's amazing what you do for these kids and you deserve to enjoy yourself." I turned to take one last look in the mirror then threw my lip gloss into my clutch. "Are you ever going to tell me the story behind why you founded this charity?"

"It's a long story, and I promise one day I'll tell you. Helping kids with HIV is just important to me. The treatments for that illness are so expensive and a lot of the kids don't live nearly as long as they should get to. If I can bring a little bit of happiness to their lives, then it's worth it."

"You're such an amazing man, you know that, right?" I asked, wrapping my arms around his neck and pushing onto my toes to kiss his neck.

"If you keep kissing me like that then we won't make it to the charity at all," he laughed as he gave me a chaste kiss and slipped his hand into mine.

CHAPTER 31

IAN

The ride to the charity event was both excruciatingly long and entirely too quick. I berated myself the entire way there for being this worked up over the possibility of seeing Maggie, but it honestly had nothing to do with her. Things with Adalyn were so amazing and I hated risking letting anything get in the way of that. Maggie was a mean, callous person and Adalyn did not deserve to be on the receiving end of that just because she's with me.

I never found out why Maggie did what she did. I never really cared to find out for myself. Once the initial shock wore off the only thing I wanted to do was thank her. It didn't matter why she hated me and treated me the way she did, it just mattered that she was finally out of my life. It hurt to think about Carrie though. How she could do that to her when Carrie had always treated her like a sister.

Carrie had been so devastated when she found out. Not just over what Maggie had done that night, but because I had never told her how Maggie treated me. Maggie was always very careful to not show her true colors in front of others and I felt I was doing the right thing by not worrying Carrie with my own personal feelings. Not to mention the fact that I spent a lot of that relationship in denial.

Adalyn had been squeezing my hand, supporting me in silence, the entire ride. I didn't even realize the limo had come to a stop in front of the hotel holding the event until Adalyn gently ran her hand down my cheek, pulling my face towards her.

"We're here."

"I'm sorry you have to see me like this. I've seen Maggie several times since that final night, and it was never difficult to just ignore her, but she's a loose canon and I don't know how she's going to react when she sees you."

"Ian, I've told you a hundred times, quit worrying about me. I'm not going anywhere, she isn't going to scare me off. If anyone will be running off scared it's her."

I gave her a nervous laugh and moved to open the door to exit the limo since the driver apparently wasn't going to do it for us.

"Hold on, one last thing before we go in," Adalyn said as she pulled on my arm. She started to undo my tie.

"Ummm…as much as I would seriously love to have sex with you in this limo, there are about twenty photographers waiting right outside this limo for us and a line of people waiting to pull up."

She laughed and shook her head at me while pulling

my tie from my collar and pushing my jacket off of my shoulders. I sat there, watching her slowly undress me, mesmerized by the excitement in her eyes. If we weren't about to have sex then why was she having me get naked?

"Adalyn…seriously, what are you doing?"

"Tonight is an important night, Ian. Important because this charity is dear to your heart, and important because this will be the first time we are out as a couple, announcing to the world that we are together. And I want to mark this special night by spending it with my boyfriend. My real boyfriend, not the pretend version of him."

"Uhhh…yeah you are just confusing me even more. You're going to have to do better than that."

As she finished unbuttoning my dress shirt and pulling it off to reveal the t-shirt I had been sporting under my suit, she slipped off my dress shoes and pulled my black converse out of a bag sitting on the seat next to her. Then she held out my suit jacket to slip my arms back through.

"You are going in there as Ian. Ian the person, brother, friend and amazing boss. Not as Ian the suit wearing, business deal making, Armani wearing robot you pretend to be," she explained as she put my own shoes on for me.

"Adalyn…I appreciate the gesture, but this is a really classy event. Everyone in there is going to be very dressed up and like it or not, I will actually look like an idiot if I go in there dressed like this. This charity is important and I need people to take me seriously if I want them to keep donating."

"People take you seriously because you are brilliant, kind and successful. You are all of those things without your suit, too, Ian," she explained as she pulled out a contacts case from the bag and handed it to me. Before I could object, she pulled out my glasses as well. "Take out your contacts and wear these, Ian. It's not a request," she giggled as she mussed up my hair.

I couldn't help laughing as I acquiesced to her demands and took out my contacts. "What about you? Won't you feel silly looking so amazing in your dress, standing next to a grown man dressed like a teenager?"

"How do you know what my dress looks like? I've had this long coat on all night, for all you know, I'm wearing a clown costume."

"Are you wearing a clown costume?"

"Well, no…I'm wearing this…" She pulled off her coat to reveal a tight fitted graphic t-shirt, similar to mine, a short plaid skirt and knee high gym socks. Pulling out a pair of Converse, matching to mine, she slipped them on and pulled her loose, wavy hair into a high ponytail. Then she slipped on glasses with thick black frames like mine to complete the look.

I couldn't hold in my laughter. "What in the world

are you wearing, Adalyn? You look like a naughty nerd straight out of a porno."

"Good, that's what I was going for," she said smugly, lifting her chin proudly in the air.

"Do you even wear glasses?"

"Well, no, but these make me look super smart, don't you think?" she giggled as she pulled them down to the tip of her nose with one hand and wiggled her eyebrows up and down.

I pulled her into my arms and kissed her long and hard, showing her with my caresses just how much I loved her for doing this.

"I don't know what I did to deserve you, but I am seriously the luckiest guy that ever lived. And even if we get laughed out of this place tonight, it will still be the best night of my life. Well, it will be the best night up until the night you say 'I Do' and become my wife."

Adalyn sucked in a sharp breath and her eyes widened in surprise. "No, don't worry, I'm not proposing right now. But don't for one second think that that won't happen soon. Very soon."

A few weeks ago a statement like that would have had Adalyn running far away from me, shutting me out entirely, but not now. She looked at me with love and admiration shining in her eyes, and all I wanted in that moment was to turn around and take her home and have her in my bed all night.

"Oh, no you don't, mister," she said as she hopped out of the limo.

"What?"

"I know that look. As turned on as I am right now, we have a party to get to. Time is of the essence, Clark Kent. Let's go."

As we approached the hotel, hand in hand, the cameras went crazy. Since Maggie, I hadn't taken a date to a single event. Any women I had chose to see, in any capacity, I had done so in private. It had given the tabloids plenty to speculate about. Was I a hopeless bachelor or a closet homosexual? Personally, I didn't care what they thought.

I did, however, care about Adalyn getting hurt. I was more than aware of how ridiculous we looked walking into a formal event dressed like characters out of a 'Revenge of the Nerds' movie, but it was hard to get too caught up in those thoughts when I had Adalyn on my arm. Whenever she was near me, the rest of the world seemed to fade away.

Still, I was showing everyone a completely different side of me. A side I had kept hidden for so long that it made me feel exposed. Years of Maggie berating me and putting me down had messed with my mind more than I had ever realized before Adalyn. Yet here I was, this amazing woman next to me, encouraging me to be whatever I wanted to be. It was liberating and for the first time in probably my entire life, I was a hundred percent comfortable with who I was.

Questions were being thrown out at us as we walked past the cameras, but Adalyn's smile never faltered. The way she squeezed my hand told me she was feeling a little overwhelmed, but it never showed on her face. She was by far the bravest person I'd ever met.

An hour passed and there was still no sign of Maggie. As happy as I was to be there with Adalyn, I couldn't help the anxiety of constantly worrying that Maggie would appear and cause a scene. I knew Adalyn was feeling neglected and I felt guilty for not giving her the attention she deserved, but I had to be prepared to intercept Maggie at any point if she did decide to show.

CHAPTER 32

ADALYN

So far that night had gone off without a hitch. Ian was the perfect example of 'geek chic' in his expensive suit paired with his converse and glasses. His tight graphic tee clung to his torso, showing off his abs in a most delicious, and lip-licking way. In about a half an hour they would lead everyone into the main banquet hall where Ian would finally get to see what Carrie and I had spent weeks planning. And as if the Gods were smiling down on me, there still had been no sighting of Maggie.

Ian had been glued to my side all night but he had been more than distracted. He kept his eyes glued to the door and had barely made eye contact with me all night. I tried not to be jealous. I knew he was doing it because he was dreading seeing her, but I couldn't help the pang of jealousy that shot through me every time he mumbled an incoherent response to something I said, clearly not listening to me.

About ten minutes before the big reveal, Ian was pulled away by a high profile client. The reluctance to leave me was clear in his face, but he had no choice. The business mogul who had stolen my date for the night took him to a far corner of the room and I eventually lost visual of him, so I let myself take in the scenery for a moment now that I was no longer solely preoccupied by Ian's anxiousness.

I immediately wished I hadn't taken a look around, because heading right for me was Maggie. I had no idea what Maggie looked like. I mean, Carrie had described her to me so I had a general idea, but I'd never seen a picture. Yet, I recognized her as soon as I saw her. The murderous glare she was giving me as soon as she walked in the door was a dead giveaway.

I was clearly her target. She wasn't even looking around for Ian or anyone else, instead she was making a beeline in my direction. Her confidence gave me pause, but I quickly gathered myself and stood a little taller, ready to put my fist in her face if that's what was necessary. When she was finally only a few feet away from me, though, her features softened. Not in a sweet, relaxed kind of way. But in an evil, up-to-no-good type of face that she must have spent hours practicing in the mirror because she was sure good at it.

"Well, well, well. Look who it is. The infamous Adalyn."

I ignored her snickering and stood stoically, determined not to give her the satisfaction of knowing how intimidated I was in that moment. It was pissing me off enough that she was even getting to me, so I'd be damned if I was going to let that her see it. Show no weakness! I proclaimed inwardly.

"Oh, not very chatty are you? Maybe you're too dumb to put together an intelligent sentence? You are pretty, but I'd imagine that's about all you have going for you if you would be willing to come to this kind of event dressed like that."

She slowly looked me up and down, not even trying to hide her disgust at my outfit. She snickered and tossed her long, red hair over her shoulder. Seriously, what had Ian ever seen in her? I guess if you had poor eyesight and weren't wearing any glasses and she was at least ten feet away then maybe she was pretty. Of course, maybe I was being overly judgmental. But screw that noise, she was ugly enough on the inside that no matter how much she dressed up the outside it didn't do any good.

"Well, I guess I really did a number on Ian if he's slumming it now. I mean, you really are the bottom of the barrel. Maybe I should take pity on Ian and let him spend the night with me. Of course, I saw what he was wearing, so we'd have to leave separately. I swear, I spend years grooming that boy and he just reverts back to his old ways as soon as I'm gone. What a waste."

I was nearing my breaking point. Holding in my pure hatred for this woman was getting harder and harder the more she spoke. I wanted to smash her teeth in. I couldn't, though. I wouldn't embarrass Ian like that. So instead I bit my tongue and clenched my fists and hoped she would eventually get bored with insulting me when she saw I wasn't going to respond and walk away.

I never got the chance to find out if that tactic would work, because Ian suddenly appeared at my side. No... wait...at her side. With his hand on the small of her back.

"Maggie, come with me please," he whispered as he lowered his head a fraction from hers, his lips almost touching her ear. She leaned toward him and let out a low moan. What the hell! Now I really wanted to tear this bitch up.

They started to walk away and I went to follow, because no way in hell was I leaving her alone with him. She had just stood there tearing me down for several minutes and I was not going to let her do that to Ian. Not tonight. Not ever again.

"Adalyn, wait here," Ian demanded coldly. The look in his eyes was dark and showed no hint of emotion. I told myself that it was not because of me, but because of Maggie being there, but seeing as how his arm was around her and not me I was having a difficult time convincing myself of that.

"Ian, I don't feel comfortable with you being alone with her. I think that..."

"No!" Ian shouted at me, taking a step in my direction. "I don't need a babysitter, Adalyn. I can take care of myself. I need to speak with Maggie alone, this does not concern you."

Then before I could blink, they were walking away

from me. Right as Ian opened the door to a dark room, Maggie turned back in my direction and winked.

What the hell just happened?

I stood there for several seconds, trying to figure out what to do. They were calling everyone into the banquet hall and my boyfriend had just ditched me for his ex and made it clear he didn't want me anywhere near them.

I thought about just going to the banquet hall and waiting for Ian at our table, but no way would my heart be able to withstand the torture of wondering when he would finally return. I had to know what was going on, and if Ian wanted me in his life, then he needed to realize that we were a team. I should be in there supporting him.

I went to turn the handle, but at the sound of Maggie's voice I decided to only open it a crack and give it a moment before I went in. I wasn't trying to spy, but if Ian really was holding his own then I wasn't going to go storming in there. His ego when it came to Maggie was already a sore spot for him and I didn't want to make it any worse if it could be avoided. So I stood watching from the small crack in the door, Ian's back was to me but I could see Maggie's face lit up by the moonlight drifting through the window they were standing only several feet away from me.

"Ian, look at you," she purred seductively, running

her hand down his arm. My body stiffened and I clinched my fists, resisting the urge to run in there and drag her away from him by her hair. Ian shrugged her hand off of him and he took one step backward, putting some distance between them. Not enough, in my opinion, but nothing other than a few continents would be enough distance in my book.

"Maggie," he replied curtly, his jaw tight and his voice cold.

"You look amazing, Ian. I'm so glad to see you looking more like your old self. I really owe you an apology." Her hand was back on his arm, but he didn't shrug her off this time. I tried to ignore that fact and continued focusing on not screaming in frustration at the woman who was blatantly flirting with my boyfriend knowing I was in the next room.

"Oh? Apologize for what, Maggie? Making me feel like shit about myself, or fucking my best friend?" Maggie winced and what looked like genuine remorse flickered in her eyes.

Best friend? Ian never told me that part. I thought we had been honest with each other about everything? Was there anything else he had kept from me? I hated the doubts that were creeping up from this line of thinking.

"For both, actually. And for not apologizing sooner. I was ashamed and I went into a deep depression for so long. I couldn't even get out of bed. By the time I had worked up the courage to maybe try and talk to you, I didn't think you'd want anything to do with me. I figured you'd rather I just stay away and I wanted to respect that."

Yeah, okay. She had just been making fun of him to me and bragging about giving him a pity fuck. This woman had to be a sociopath.

"Apology accepted, Maggie. Now if you'll excuse me…" Ian trailed off as he started to turn away from her, but before he had made it even one step, Maggie grabbed him by the arm. He spun around to face her but again didn't pull from her grip.

I suddenly felt like the intruder I knew I was, but I couldn't bring myself to leave. Why wasn't he pulling away from her? Did he have a plan? I knew men weren't supposed to hit women, but surely that rule could be looked aside in Maggie's case.

"Please, Ian, let me apologize properly. It's why I came tonight. I needed to see you. I just need five minutes of your time. Please." She was begging, not even trying to hide the desperation in her voice. From everything I'd been told about her, I assumed this was some sort of game or manipulation, and surely Ian would see through that.

Why would he even entertain the thought of talking to her? Why had he come into this room with her in the first place? I assumed he had brought her in here to yell at her, tell her where to shove it, tell her he hated her. He hadn't done any of that so far. I was starting to feel sick to my stomach. This wasn't right. This whole scene playing out before me was just…wrong.

"Ian, please. We were together for six years. I was your fiancé. Surely you can find it in your heart to give me just a few minutes. Just a few minutes and I promise I'll walk away if that's what you want."

Fiancé?! What?!

No. That can't be right. Surely Ian would have told me that part. This must be another game. Ian is going to tell her she's crazy and walk away. He will have her and her crazy ass thrown out and we will go back to how it was before, before she showed up and ruined everything I'd been planning for tonight. Any second now, he will tell her to go to hell. Any second.

Only that didn't happen. Instead, as Ian nodded his head, but instead of talking, Maggie launched herself at him. All I could see were her suddenly exposed breasts and one arm wrapped around his neck while she pressed her free hand to his crotch, stroking him through his pants. A moan escaped Ian's mouth and I stumbled backwards.

It only took all of two seconds for me to decide what I was doing and I shoved open the door again and cleared my throat. Their faces pulled apart and Ian looked over his shoulder looking confused and then afraid as it reg-

istered who it was that had walked in on their little…
moment. Maggie was still stroking him over his pants,
giving me a smirk that made me want to set her on fire.
Someone give me some gasoline and a freaking match!

Ian just stood there, frozen, not saying anything and
not even bothering to push Maggie away. All my resolve
left me at once and the scene before me finally sank in.
The man I love, caught with his ex-girlfriend… no…
ex-fiancé, and he wasn't even bothering to make up an
excuse.

I felt as if the whole world was crashing down on
me. My chest was literally splitting open. I wanted the
floor to open up and swallow me whole. Before I could
stop it an angry sob spilled out from between my lips
and the dams burst, flooding my eyes in tears. I couldn't
breathe. I literally felt like I was suffocating, like the
pain in my chest was strangling me.

Even if Ian did try to explain in that moment, it
wouldn't matter. There was no logical explanation as to
what was happening. He finally jerked away from her as
if just realizing what was happening and started to move
toward me, but I took a matching step backwards.

It was done. It was over. I'd finally given myself to
someone, heart, body and soul, and he forgot me as soon
as someone else walked in.

"Adalyn, wait!" He yelled for me, but it was too
late. I was already moving.

I ran. Ran out of the lobby, past all of the camera crews outside, past the limo driver who yelled something as I broke out into a dead sprint. I didn't know where I was running, but it didn't matter, as long as it was far away from Ian.

CHAPTER 33

IAN

"Stacy! Carrie!" I burst into the banquet hall, scanning the room for anyone who could help me. I couldn't even think about what it was going to take to get Adalyn to understand what had just happened, but after running after her and not spotting her anywhere, I decided reinforcements were necessary.

I yelled again, interrupting a speaker at the podium and causing every head to turn in my direction. It was only then I realized that there were pictures of me all over the room. Life size posters, banners hanging from the ceiling, promotional posters lining the walls.

What the hell?

"Ah! The man of the hour!" Bill, my vice president of game development yelled from the podium. "Please, Ian! Join us!"

Clapping and cheering ensued but I couldn't go up there right now. I needed to find Adalyn. Screw my job. Nothing was important without her. I didn't have a choice though as two employees hoisted me up on their shoulders and led me up to the stage.

Seriously, what the hell was happening?

They sat me down on my feet next to Bill, and he slapped me on the back and shook my hand vigorously.

"So, where's your lovely woman who made all this happen?"

It took me a second to realize he was speaking to me and that he was asking about Adalyn. How did I answer that question? I had no idea where she was. And what did he mean made all of this happen? What was this?

"Ahem," I cleared my throat, trying to think of an excuse. "She had an emergency come up. She's very sorry."

"Oh, well that's a shame. I know how much she was looking forward to doing the big reveal herself."

The confusion on my face must have been obvious because he let out a full belly laugh and explained.

"Adalyn came to me a few weeks ago with an idea for a comic book series and we loved it. Loved it so much we are also turning it into a video game and even possibly a television series. It's a spin off of the Superman and Batman storylines. Normal, everyday Joe by day, then at night or when in need, he strips off his designer suit to become the town's superhero. As you can see, the character is loosely based off of you. Very close in appearance and his name is Drake even. The only detail we have yet to work out is his superhero name. Adalyn wanted to leave that up to you."

My head was drowning with all of this information. Did he just say Adalyn had based a comic book and video game off of me? The appearance of the character was more than similar; it was practically a mirror image.

Is this what she had been working on for weeks with Carrie? I knew they were working on developing something and she wouldn't tell me what it was, but she was so excited to be back at work I didn't want to hound her for more information.

She had gone to all this trouble to do this for me, probably because she knew how nervous I was about tonight, and I had gone and been the biggest dumbass in the history of all dumbasses.

I needed to find her. I needed to explain. I mumbled an apology and ran off the stage.

Stacy and Carrie met me at the door, confused and angry faces stopping me in my tracks. They each yanked me by an arm and dragged me into the lobby.

"What the hell, Ian! Where is Adalyn?" Stacy was yelling.

"I don't know, okay!? I need you to help me find her." I was frantic and starting to panic. The look on her face before she ran out, the look that told her she clearly believed I had betrayed her...

"What do you mean you don't know, Ian? What the hell is going on?" Carrie yelled, joining in on the hysteria.

"She walked in on me and Maggie and she freaked out and ran out of the building. I went after her but she was already gone. She won't answer her phone and I don't know where she went."

Suddenly a punch landed on my right shoulder, and it hurt like a mother fucker.

"What the hell, Carrie? Where did you learn to punch like that?" Before she could answer, Stacy punched me equally as hard on my other arm. "Dammit! Stop it!"

"Listen, brother. I don't know what you mean by 'walked in on you and Maggie' and don't for a second think you won't be explaining that shit later. But right now we need to go find Adalyn. She's probably devastated and not thinking rationally so we need to get to her before something bad happens."

We rushed out of the building, my mind racing, trying to think of where Adalyn might have run off to, all the while being cussed out by a very angry Stacy, close on my heels.

CHAPTER 34

ADALYN

I had no idea what time it was. Had no idea where I was or how long I'd been walking once I had been forced to stop running once my lungs started screaming for air. If I hadn't feared I would pass out if I didn't stop, I would have just kept running. The fire emanating from my lungs throughout my chest was much more tolerable than my heart feeling like it was literally dying.

I didn't have my phone or any money, so I couldn't even get a hold of someone to come pick me up, so I just kept walking. My body was screaming at me to stop moving, to let it rest for a few minutes, but I couldn't. If I stopped moving, then the images of Ian wrapped up in another woman would consume me. The only way I was keeping them at bay was by focusing on the pain that radiated through every muscle of my body the longer I walked.

I finally had an idea of what time it was when the sun started to rise. That meant I'd been walking for at least eight hours straight. No wonder every inch of my body was so fatigued. My feet had blisters and my eyes burned from exhaustion and crying, even though the tears had dried up a couple of hours ago. I was severely dehydrated and my stomach was churning, but I didn't care.

By this point I wasn't even in the city any more. I was walking along some side road, leading God knows where. I hadn't passed a gas station or any kind of civilization for at least a few miles and I wondered briefly if I might actually die out here. There hadn't been a single car since I started down this road and if no one found me soon then I might actually die, or at the very least, end up in the hospital.

And when the thought of dying actually brought more relief than the thought of having to turn back, I turned to the bushes next to the road and retched. Anything left in my system was violently expelled as I realized just how broken I was.

Even after the rape I'd never thought about ending my life. Not that I was thinking of killing myself, but the fact that death sounded appealing right now told me just how far gone I was. It had taken me years…years…to find myself again after the rape. I honestly didn't think I could recover from this.

As I stood there, dry heaving on the side of the road, entertaining the most morbid thoughts I'd ever had in my life, I suddenly heard a car approaching slowly.

I turned to see a police officer pulling up alongside the road, his lights on but the sirens off. When he got out of his car I thought I recognized him, but I was so weak and my vision was so blurry that I couldn't make out the details of his face. He approached me cautiously, as if I were a wounded wild animal he intended to capture.

"Adalyn?" He asked once he was only a couple feet from where I was still hunched over, clutching my stomach. I tried to nod, but suddenly my body just gave out and everything got blurry as I started to fall to the ground. I felt strong arms catch me and I faintly remember crying out Ian's name, right before everything went black.

CHAPTER 35

IAN

"Stacy, you have to let me see her. I have to see her. I need to explain!" I was frantic, pacing back and forth in the waiting room of the hospital where Adalyn had been admitted.

"No way, Ian. She doesn't want to see you, and I can't say I blame her. To be honest with you, you're lucky I don't jack your shit up right here. The only reason I haven't ripped off your testicles is because I'm giving you the benefit of the doubt. But if you give me any reason at all to believe that what Adalyn saw is anywhere close to the truth, I swear to you, you'll leave this hospital a woman because you will have been castrated."

"Dammit, Stacy, of course what she saw isn't what it looked like. There is an explanation and I'll be happy to explain it to you, but I need to explain it to Adalyn first. She needs to be the first one to hear it and soon, Stacy. She's hurting. I know she's hurting. I need to fix this."

I'd left my pride back in that damn ballroom. I didn't care what amount of begging and pleading it would take to get Adalyn to listen to me, I would do whatever it took. I knew it looked horrible. I can only imagine what was running through Adalyn's mind right now, how confused and hurt she must be and it was eating me alive.

"Look, Ian, for what it's worth, I'm sorry. But I can't let you go in there without her permission. The doctors said she should be able to go home sometime today most likely. Maybe she will be willing to see you once she's out of the hospital."

"It's been three days, Stacy. THREE. DAYS. She's been sick and hurting for three days. The longer she goes without giving me a chance to explain, the longer she is in pain. The further she drifts away from me. You know how hard it is to get through to her, Stacy. If I don't get to talk to her soon she will have already shut me out completely, and I don't know if I'll ever be able to get her to let me back in."

"So what, if Adalyn keeps refusing to see you, you're just going to give up? If it's too hard you'll just cut your losses? Go back to that bitch of an ex?"

"Stop it, Stacy! You know that's not true! Adalyn is it for me. Whether she ever takes me back or not, it doesn't matter. There is no one else for me. I'll spend every day the rest of my life trying to prove to her that I am the man she fell in love with and that what she saw was a mistake. I would never hurt her. Not intentionally."

"Really? Well you did a damn good job of doing it accidentally, so I'd hate to see what you would have done to her if it had been on purpose. Aside from murder I'm not sure how you would even top this, anyway."

"Dammit!" I was going to go bald from yanking on my hair as much as I had been. I hadn't been home, hadn't eaten and had only passed out for a few minutes at a time since Adalyn had been admitted to the hospital.

Thank God that cop had found her on the side of the road. I can't even bring myself to think of what might have happened if she had been out there alone too much longer. The doctor's said she was severely dehydrated and was unconscious when she first arrived to the emergency room. Once she had woken up, she had been hysterical, ripping out her IV and scratching at her skin. Stacy said the doctor's had to sedate her when she wouldn't stop screaming.

I was afraid they were going to admit her into the psych ward, but she eventually calmed down. They were still thinking of admitting her because she still hadn't spoken a word. The only person she would acknowledge was Stacy and even then she hadn't communicated anything verbally. The only reason they were considering letting her leave now was because Stacy had signed a waiver agreeing to take responsibility for watching her over the next week. She was even taking an entire week off of work because they recommended Adalyn not be alone.

I hated that all of this information was second hand. I hated that Stacy was going to be the one taking care of Adalyn when I wanted it to be me. When Adalyn shouldn't even have to be taken care of like this because I never should have hurt her in the first place. I knew we never should have gone to that charity event. I had no doubt that Maggie would cause trouble, but I never imagined I would have any hand in it. I was so mad and I had nowhere to direct my anger at but myself.

I never should have even spoken to Maggie. I should have taken Adalyn's hand and walked away. I especially should have never walked off with Maggie. I just needed to get her away from Adalyn. I knew she wouldn't leave us alone until I let her say her peace and I was trying to spare Adalyn from whatever lies and hate came spewing out of Maggie's mouth.

I'd never regretted something so much in my entire life. The thought of losing Adalyn was unbearable.

No. No. I couldn't think like that. I would get Adalyn back. I would explain everything and it would be hard but she would trust me again eventually and we could go back to where we were. I loved Adalyn. We were meant to be together. As clichéd as that sounded, it was true. I never felt more right than when Adalyn was in my arms. Maybe it sounded like codependency that I knew I couldn't go on without her. That I needed her more than I needed to breathe, but I didn't care. It was true. There was no life for me anymore without Adalyn. Not a life worth living, anyway.

"Stacy, please. I'm desperate. I'll do anything. You

know I love her. You know this is killing me. I need you to trust me, even though you have no reason to right now, but I need you to. You saw what I went through with Maggie and you know I would never do that to someone else. I would never hurt Adalyn like that. I'd leave her before I'd cheat."

Stacy sighed and hung her head. She was just as exhausted as me. She had only left the hospital a couple of times to run get things for Adalyn and do some necessary errands, but other than that she hadn't left Adalyn's side. She was an amazing friend and I would be forever grateful to her for being there for Adalyn through all of this.

"I know, Ian. I just don't know what you want me to do. The one time I said your name she freaked out. They almost had to sedate her again. She's just been through so much. She didn't even break down like this after she was raped. It's like something snapped in her this time. I think the weight of all the pain she's been harboring all these years just came barreling at her when she saw you with Maggie. I don't think everything she's feeling right now is entirely your fault, some of it just residual emotions from her past that she's channeling on to you, but I really think you just need to respect her wishes right now and keep your distance. I promise, as soon as I think she can handle talking to you, I'll call you. That's the best I can do."

I knew she was right. It was killing me not being

able to talk to her, hold her, make all her pain go away, but seeing me right now would most likely make it worse.

"I'm not really supposed to repeat any of this and Adalyn would probably be mad at me for how much I've been telling you, but believe it or not, I want you guys to work out," Stacy said in almost a whisper, staring at the ground.

"What is it, Stacy? What did they say?" I begged, grabbing her shoulders and urging her to look at me, pleading with my eyes.

Her shoulders slumped and she stalked towards one of the seats in the waiting area, putting her head in her hands with her elbows resting on her knees. When she finally looked up at me, she had tears running down her cheeks.

"Stacy please, you're killing me here. You never cry. It can't be good if you're crying. Just tell me, please. I can handle it."

She took in a shaky breath and exhaled deeply. "The doctors said they think she is having some kind of post traumatic event. Apparently her psychiatrist she saw after the rape had predicted this sort of thing, claiming Addy never fully accepted what had happened to her. Her doctor had spent months trying to get her to truly face what had happened, but she was coping in all the wrong ways and her doctor wrote that there was a good possibility that another traumatic event in her life might have this kind of backlash." She paused, taking in another shaky breath.

"They called her psychiatrist and he actually flew out here yesterday and saw her. He confirmed that that's what is happening to her. And he…" Stacy trailed off, looking everywhere but at me.

"What Stacy, just say it."

"He said he recommends Adalyn not see you. That since what happened with you is what triggered her episode, that she may now associate you with the rape and it could send her into hysterics again. He said that…" Stacy trailed off again as she wiped a tear from her face. "He said that she may never fully recover, and that even if she does, she may never be able to see you and react normally. I'm so sorry, Ian. I don't know how much of that is true. Maybe he's a quack. Maybe he's just exaggerating and giving the worst case scenario. I'm sure with time it will be fine. Adalyn is strong, she can get through this."

I couldn't hear anything else Stacy said after that. It was too much to take in, the thought of Adalyn associating me with so much pain and grief. The thought that every time she saw my face that it would bring so much pain that she would fall apart. How could I fix things if that were true? Nothing I said or did would be able to undo that kind of damage.

I needed air. I couldn't breathe, it felt like the walls

were closing in on me. I just needed to be anywhere else right then. And without another look back, I walked out.

CHAPTER 36

ADALYN

I didn't know how long it had been since that horrible night. The night my life officially ended. Metaphorically, of course. I still hadn't spoken to anyone. I knew it was killing Stacy. She eventually went back to work once she realized I wasn't going to do anything crazy like slit my wrists or something. I think when I finally started eating solid foods is when she felt comfortable enough to leave me alone for a while, though she was only working half days.

I was getting damn tired of being baby sat. I appreciated what she was doing for me, and I wasn't mad at her, I was mad at myself. I wasn't sitting around feeling sorry for myself anymore. I hadn't talked because I truly had nothing worth saying. I wasn't ready to pretend like everything was okay and I definitely was not ready to talk about what happened. So I just didn't talk.

I knew I needed to snap out of this soon before I completely pushed everyone away from me for good. Carrie hadn't been to visit in at least two days now. I guess she realized it was pointless since I didn't talk or make eye contact. I couldn't even imagine what must be going through everyone's minds right then. They must have thought I was out of my mind. Literally. I'm sure I looked it.

I was showering and going through the daily motions, mostly doing things out of muscle memory rather
than actual effort. I was going to have to leave the apartment soon because being cooped up was making things
worse, I knew, but it would be harder to not speak out in
public. Strangers expected eye contact and polite words
and I could provide neither. Not that I cared what people
thought, but I didn't want to be rude just because I was
a mess.

I'd stopped playing that night over and over in my
head. I realized a few days in that torturing myself by
having the memory of Ian's hands on her was not making anything better. It was bad enough what he had done
to me, but to keep reliving it over and over was no one's
fault but my own.

It was hard to keep myself distracted at first. I had
no interest in doing anything at all. Sounds annoyed me
and every time I tried to watch TV or listen to music I
just became increasingly agitated. I tried reading but I
couldn't focus long enough to make it past a few pages.
So I did a lot of mundane tasks. I cleaned, organized,
cooked. Even when there was nothing to do, I'd clean
everything again or I'd bake dozens of cookies and vari-
ous treats. Stacy lectured me constantly about how fat
she was going to get, and I'd never admit it to her, but
her nagging me as if everything were normal was exactly

what I needed.

One morning after Stacy left for work I was looking for something to do and decided to bake something since I'd already cleaned every nook and cranny of the apartment at least three times in the last couple of days. Only when I started to gather all the ingredients, I noticed we were missing several. I thought about texting Stacy and asking her to pick them up on her way home from work, but decided against it. I could handle going to the store, it would be good for me to get out and get some air.

I didn't want to have to talk to a cab driver and tell them where to go, so I decided to walk the seven blocks to the grocery store. I kept my head down and stayed as far off the sidewalk as I could to avoid running in to anyone. It wasn't until someone collided directly into me, almost knocking me into the street, that I finally looked up.

I wished I hadn't. I wished I had just let a cab run over me right there on the street, because standing directly in front of me was Maggie.

Weeks of pent up emotions came barreling out at once. Something about the smirk on her face just made me snap, and before I could even figure out what I was doing, my fist was making contact with her jaw. A small amount of blood splattered out of her mouth and onto the ground, and I saw red. I knocked her to the ground and started pounding on her face, relentless in my punches.

I couldn't stop if I wanted to, even though I didn't want to. Her face was covered in blood by the time someone finally intervened.

My body was being pulled off of hers as I kicked and screamed, trying to get loose and finish my assault. I spit in her face and continued to call her names as someone dragged me further away and then pulled me into the back seat of a car.

I was still so blinded by my rage that it took me several seconds to even realize where I was. When it registered that I'd been pulled into a car by a stranger, I panicked and immediately thought I was in the back of a police cruiser, but as I took in my surroundings I realized I was in the back of a town car. Before I could make a move to get out, the door on the opposite side opened and someone slid in.

Ian.

I wanted to be angry. I wanted to scream and attack him like I had Maggie, but his expression gave me pause. I sucked in a sharp breath and took in his appearance.

"You look like shit," I said before I could stop myself, then I smacked my hand over my mouth in surprise. Then I officially lost it. I started laughing. Laughing so hard I couldn't breathe, my stomach muscles aching from the strain of being used for the first time in weeks. The confused look on Ian's face only made me laugh harder, and even as it registered exactly what was happening, I couldn't stop. I should be angry, yelling at him, freaking out even. Not laughing.

"Adalyn, are you okay?" His tone was cautious and you could tell he was trying to figure out what to do.

"I'm sorry," I said between laughs and gasps for air. "I don't know why I'm laughing so hard. It's just…I just beat the shit out of someone. I've never hit anyone in my life! Well besides Stacy. I haven't even spoken a word in weeks and then all of a sudden I just…I just…attack someone!" I was bent over clutching my stomach, my cheeks starting to hurt from smiling so much.

Suddenly the smile Ian had been fighting back as he tried to get a read on me broke free and he joined in my laughter. I don't know how long we sat there cracking up in the back of his car, but it felt so good to feel something other than anger and hopelessness that I couldn't bring myself to stop.

Eventually the laughter started to die down, and I laid my head back against the seat, exhausted. I let my head roll to the side, and really took in Ian's appearance. He really did look horrible. He'd lost weight, his clothes hanging off of his body. His clothes were wrinkled and looked as if he'd been wearing them several days in a row. He had big bags under his eyes, and his eyes looked sunken in, giving his face a hollow look. And despite the smile still lingering on his face, his eyes just looked sad.

It hit me like a ton of bricks that I was in a car with

Ian. Like a punch to the gut I came back to reality. I remembered I should be angry and for a split second I considered just jumping out of the car, even though it was moving. But I didn't want to. Despite the pain I felt being near Ian, I also felt at peace for the first time in weeks. I missed him. I missed him so much it hurt. Hurt more than the pain of what he'd done.

"Why, Ian? Why would you do that to me?"

CHAPTER 37

IAN

I was temporarily stunned into silence. I had rehearsed in my head a thousand times what I would say to Adalyn when I had the chance. Not because any of it was untrue, but because I was afraid I would only get one shot at explaining myself and I didn't want to mess it up. Only I was messing it up, because I wasn't saying anything at all.

The last half hour had just been so bizarre; it had completely thrown me. When I saw Adalyn on top of Maggie, beating her to a bloody pulp, I reacted instinctively. I couldn't give a shit what happened to Maggie, but I knew the cops would show up soon and the last thing Adalyn needed right now was to be hauled off to jail.

Then when I got into the car I expected her to hit me or scream at me or just get out and run. I never expected her to start laughing. Seeing her like that, smiling and bent over laughing, it was the first time since that day at the hospital that I felt a glimmer of hope.

And here was my chance. Adalyn was looking at me patiently, still breathing heavily from laughing so hard. She looked so beautiful and I wanted so badly to pull her into my arms to hold her and never let go. I asked my driver to pull over and step out to give us a moment of privacy.

"I'm sorry, Adalyn," I said lamely. I shook my head in embarrassment, knowing I was messing this up. I was just so terrified of doing or saying the wrong thing that I couldn't pull together a coherent sentence.

And just when I thought Adalyn couldn't surprise me any more, she reached over and took my hand in hers and said, "I know."

"You know?"

"I know you're sorry. I've had a lot of time to think over the past few weeks and I know there has to be some logical explanation about what happened, I just wasn't ready to hear it yet. Even if you don't want to be with me Ian…even if you'd rather go back to her…I still know you didn't do what you did to hurt me. And if what you want is to be with her, I'll let you go. I just…I need to know why."

I never felt more unworthy of her love than in that moment. How the doctors ever thought she wouldn't recover is beyond me. She is by far the strongest person I have ever met.

"Oh my God, Adalyn, no. I mean, yes, I didn't mean to hurt you. But no, I don't want Maggie. I know how it looked. I know it looked horrible and I wish so badly that I could go back and do things differently so that you wouldn't have to live with that horrible image in your head, but I can't and so I can promise you I'll spend the rest of my life giving you as many amazing images as it takes to get that one out of your head."

"Ian," she said patiently. "Just tell me what happened. Please."

"Okay, well, I guess I should start at the beginning. The first thing I should apologize for is for not telling you that the person Maggie cheated on me with was my best friend."

"Yeah…why would you leave something like that out?"

"Because he was also Carrie's boyfriend at the time. That part was harder on her than it was me and I didn't want to share that part because it's more important to her story than mine. I figured that detail would get brought up eventually and I wanted to give Carrie the chance to tell you on her own terms before I said anything."

Adalyn squeezed my hand in response and gave me a sympathetic smile, encouraging me to keep going.

"Either way, I still should have told you and for that I'm sorry. As for her saying she was my fiancé…" I paused, giving Adalyn a chance to speak, but she continued to sit patiently, waiting for my explanation.

"I asked her to marry me that night, the night she cheated on me. I asked her before we ever left for the event, but she just said she needed to think about it and didn't even take the ring. I hadn't made a big deal about it. I'm not proud of it, but I bought the first ring I saw without any thought, and when I asked her I didn't even get down on one knee. We'd just been together for so long and it seemed like the next step in my life and I felt some sort of strange obligation to do it, but my heart wasn't in it. When she didn't give me an answer right away I wasn't even upset, I was just relieved. I never should have been with her. I should have ended it long before it ever came to that, I know that now."

"Then what happened in that room, Ian? I saw all of it. I'm sorry that I spied, but that's not what I had intended to do initially. I was just worried about you. You snapped at me...you'd never spoken to me like that before. Maggie had been running her mouth, saying all kinds of hateful things, and I didn't want her to turn that on you and ruin the evening. But if you don't still love her, then why were your hands all over her? I heard a moan, Ian. You moaned, and that's when I..." She choked on her words and started to pull her hand away, but I grabbed onto her and tugged lightly, pulling her closer to me.

"I took her in there to yell at her. She is always playing games and when I saw her over there talking to you, I knew she had to be saying awful things. Your fists were clenched and you seriously looked like you wanted to kill her. I panicked and pulled her into that room so that when I laid into her for harassing you it wouldn't cause a scene. I'm so sorry for snapping at you, there is no excuse for me doing that. All I can tell you is that I was already so ready to yell at her that when you tried to step in, I overreacted and let my pride get in the way. I didn't want you or her thinking I couldn't handle it by myself, and you offering to help in that moment made me feel weak. I know now how stupid and selfish that kind of reaction was, but I wasn't thinking rationally."

I paused, grinding my teeth and trying to push down the fury that rose at the thought of Maggie and how she had the nerve to come back into my life and try to mess with me again. "When we got in the room, she spoke before I had a chance and just the sound of her voice brought up so many horrible memories… It took everything I had not to hit her, took so much strength not to physically harm a woman and that thought made me feel ashamed. So for a minute I froze, trying to decide if I was going to be able to yell at her without hitting her or if I should just walk away."

I took in Adalyn's face, trying to get a read on what she was feeling, but she showed nothing. She either had a really good poker face or there was really no judgment coming from her. She should be judging me. I was weak. I should have been able to keep my composure and put Maggie in her place for having the nerve to approach Adalyn.

"Your timing was impeccable. In that moment when

she was begging me to stay and talk to her, I thought that maybe if I just let her say whatever she needed to say then she would just leave us alone, let it all go. When I thought of you in the other room waiting on me, I realized she wasn't even worth my time. She wasn't worth the energy it would take to yell at her, I should have just thrown her out. So right as I found my voice and started to tell her to just leave, she yanked her dress down and threw herself at me. I went to push her off me but then her hand was on my...you know...and it shocked me just long enough for her to lock me in. It all happened so fast, and before I had a chance to push her away you were there. I know you probably don't believe me," I said, shaking my head. "But it's true. I would never do that to you, Adalyn. I would never do to anyone what she did to me. I feel nothing for her. Nothing emotional or physical. I only see you, I only want you. When she touched me it was repulsive. Feeling her mouth on mine..." My whole body shuddered at the memory. "If you hadn't walked in when you did I think I might have literally thrown up on her."

Adalyn barked out a laugh, and when I finally forced myself to look up at her, it was clear she believed me. I didn't deserve it, I didn't know why she believed me, but I had never been so relieved in my life.

"I'm sorry, Ian."

"What!?" I yelled a little too loudly. Of all the responses I anticipated, her apologizing was not one of them.

"I'm sorry. I'm sorry for not trusting you. For reacting before I gave you a chance to explain. For running off like that and worrying you and then pushing you away for so long. I know how much that must have hurt you, and it wasn't fair of me to punish you because of my sordid past, and for that I am really, truly sorry. I saw it all, the whole thing. Everything you're saying matches up with what I saw and I believe you. I really do. Do you think that you could forgive me?"

I took a moment to really look at Adalyn, wondering how it was possible for someone to be so perfect. Instead of hating me like she should or refusing to believe me, she was worried about me forgiving her?

"No, I won't forgive you Adalyn, because you did absolutely nothing wrong. I hold all the blame. And by the way…the comic book? What was that all about?"

A mischievous grin spread across her face and she cupped the side of my face in her palm. "You're my hero, Ian. When I didn't think I needed saving, you saved me any way. I didn't realize how much pain I was still in until you. How much I was missing in life by closing myself off like I had been. You pressed and pressed for more of me…you never gave up no matter how much I pushed you away. I could never thank you for everything you've done for me, just by loving me. I wanted to show you and I got the idea that first night when you took off your dress shirt and had that Superman t-shirt on. So I asked Carrie to help me and almost the entire company was involved. They all agree that your kindness, generosity and willingness to sacrifice yourself for others makes you as close to a hero as anyone, and they were excited to help."

I couldn't believe Adalyn and so many people had gone so far out of their way to do something like that for me. I didn't know what to say.

"That's amazing, Adalyn. But why the charity fundraiser? Why was that the night of the big reveal?"

An even bigger grin took over her face and her eyes lit up like it was Christmas morning.

"That's the best part," she said giddily. "All the proceeds from all of that will go directly to the Drake Foundation. So not only are you still helping so many people in the ways you already had been, but this comic book and whatever else we turn it into that is specifically inspired by you, will help even more."

Before she could say another word I pulled her the rest of the way into my lap, twining my fingers through her hair and hungrily kissed her as if it was the last time I would ever get to feel her soft lips on mine. She moaned in response, returning my kiss with the same amount of hunger as she started pulling on the hem of my shirt, lifting it over my head.

"I've missed you so much," she said as she trailed kisses down my neck and to my stomach, where she was hastily undoing the button to my jeans.

As much as I wanted her, and I really wanted her, she deserved more than a quick fuck in the back of a car after everything we had been through. So I took her face in my hands, cupping both her cheeks as I kissed her softly.

"I've missed you too, more than you'll ever know. And I want you so badly, but not here. Not like this. I want you in my bed, where I can take my time with you. I want to worship you, taste every inch of you, and make sweet love to you until neither of us have the strength to move. I want to memorize every curve of your body and hold you in my arms all night. Tell me you want that, too, Adalyn."

She looked longingly into my eyes and I knew in that moment that we could overcome anything, and there wasn't a doubt in my mind that soon...very soon...this beautiful woman would be my wife.

ACKNOWLEDGEMENTS

So many people to thank! First off, anyone who decided to give my book a chance and read it, THANK YOU! Secondly, thank you to my husband and his unwavering support. When I set out to do this I had no idea what I was doing and wasn't even sure if I could accomplish it. I couldn't have made this happen without you, mister! I'd also like to thank my best friend, Stacy. Stacy not only supported me, encouraged me and helped me through every step of this process, but she was also the real life inspiration for book Stacy. I also want to thank all of my friends and family who read this book before I published, providing me with feedback and encouragement. Missy, Monica, Susie, Teresa - thank you for helping! Lastly I want to thank the amazing authors who inspired me to do this, especially those who helped me throughout the process. NA Alcorn, Stacy Kestwick and Morgan Rayne. Your words of wisdom are more appreciated than you know.